The Reluctant Mountaineer

Betsy Goodspeed

2nd Printing by Instantpublisher.com
Copyright © Dec. 2004 Betsy Goodspeed
Published by HOME2MEDIA
Betsytryanglesbcglobal.net

ISBN 1-59196-617-5

For my grandchildren

And their children

And their children

Chapter One

June, 1979
Pinecrest Camp, Wyoming

Charlie Barnes issued a stern order, "Mickey, for the last time, fasten the belt of that lifejacket! I'm not going to tell you again."

Mickey argued, "It doesn't fit me, Dad. It's too little."

Chuck razzed him with older brother superiority, "Well, loosen it, dumb-bell."

"Darn it all, how?" Usually Mickey answered Chuck's meanness with sarcasm, but his sense of humor had taken a beating in the last few days.

1

He thought to himself *'why did there have to be family vacations anyway?* Why couldn't Dad and Chuck go camping by themselves and Mom have some time off from cooking meals and washing clothes? Then he could have hung around home to watch TV and read comic books, or gone over to Hodge's house where no one would make cracks about his laziness.

He fought with the life-belt buckle and ranted silently. Why did Randy's dad have to be such a grouch? If Mr. Hodge had been willing to let him and Randy split their time between the Barnes' house and Hodge's they could have had a real vacation of their own instead of being dragged on their father's vacations! He gritted his teeth and vowed that when he got to be sixteen he would be in charge of his own life!

"What are you doing, son?" His father was already out of patience with him and the vacation was only starting. "That belt works exactly like the one on your Scout uniform. You can figure that out, I'm sure."

Seventeen-year-old Chuck teased, "Too much baby fat?" Then his attention shifted to more important things and he urged, "Dad, let's row over to the other side of the river. The fishing's bound to be better away from the crowds camped on this side."

"You're right, Chuck," his father approved. "Trying to catch anything here would only result in having canned beans for supper."

He struck out with the oars and told the dog beside him, "Balance the boat, Sport."

Chuck's Golden Retriever scrambled aft in the confident way of a dog accustomed to boat rides and Mickey grumbled peevishly at him, "Will you get outa' my way, you big floor mop?"

He blew dog hair out of his mouth and wished that his mom hadn't made him go fishing. Chuck's precious hunting dog was better at fishing than a landlubber who would rather eat baked beans than stinky fish any day of the week. Besides, Dad and Chuck didn't want him along anyway

Chuck suggested, "Get Sport to fasten your life preserver for you, Mick. He's smart enough to do that."

"I'm getting it," Mickey muttered darkly. "Just tell your big ape-hound to move his fat butt outa' my way."

Now he wished that he had learned to swim. Having to strap on the bright orange jacket was an advertisement to the whole camp that he was a Class A dumb-bell.

His dad was so determined to make an outdoor man out of his fourteen-year-old observer. During the long, boring drive through Wyoming he had said that the sooner Mickey accepted that necessity the better off he would be.

Mickey argued in his mind that there were lots of people, Mr. Hodge, for example, who never went camping. They made a good living and they were respected. Making money was what counted. It didn't even matter whether a guy went to college. Why didn't his dad know that?

There was only one way that belt would let his fingers loosen it enough to buckle it. He had to stand up for five seconds so his stomach could pull in. He rocked forward and the boat lurched as he managed to get to his feet.

"Sit down!" Chuck yelped and made a frantic grab for him. The boat tipped further and he gasped, "Mick --"

Mickey didn't have time to think, much less change his mind about which way to fall. He went headfirst into the cold water with his hands still trying to hook the belt.

The swift current pulled him away from the boat, then below the surface. His hands beat at the water in a desperate attempt to swim, but the swirling force pulled him down again. The lifejacket rising to his shoulders kept him from being able to use his hands, and then the bulky jacket floated away and there was nothing to hold onto.

3

Before he went down for the third time he heard Chuck shout, "No, Dad, don't jump! That's a deathtrap down there! Sport, stay!"

The deathtrap pulled Mickey into a surging hole with high walls of suffocating water. Holding his breath was instinctive and fear paralyzed him. He shut his eyes tightly and his astounded brain whispered '*Am I going to die? Is that possible? To be alive one minute and then not alive?*'

His chest swelled to bursting, his ears were ready to explode from the pressure building in his head and his legs were being pulled down as if ropes were attached to his ankles. His cramping body rolled into a ball with his arms crossed over his rigid chest and his brain wanted to scream with pain and terror. Then he couldn't hold his breath any longer and he gulped in water -- a spasmodic gasp, and then another. He thought '*I'm drowning. That's all there is... my life is over before it really started.*'

Consciousness departed and the beginning of death softened pain and anger. Even fear floated away in misty, drifting sleep.

The tunnel he was pulled through was warm and blessedly dry. His body felt like it was wrapped in lightweight quilts and the stillness was deep and velvet. Then the silence became alive with hope and he saw a welcoming light ahead. A golden glow surrounded him and he stood beside someone very kind who drew him close to let him know that he wouldn't be alone or unloved in this place.

Just as he was feeling relieved that death was not going to be so terrible after all, he felt himself being drawn away from the warmth of the kind person who had welcomed him to the fringes of eternity.

He begged, "No, don't send me back, I want to stay." But his prayer was choked off in his tight throat and he woke up coughing foul-tasting water onto a rocky surface that bruised his face and forced him back to reality.

Something alive and fleshy licked a large, flat tongue at his face. He gasped, "Ukh!" and his hands pushed weakly at the monstrous hairy creature that stood braced over him with its horrible tongue drooling into his eyes.

Sportin' Life barked. The piercing sound echoed in Mickey's ears and he mumbled with relief, "Stupid animal, you were told to stay."

Looking around to find out where they were, he found that it was almost too dark too see anything. They seemed to have been pulled through the watery tunnel to an underground cavern with walls carved of stone. He guessed that Sport must have dragged him out of the water onto the bank because he had no memory of getting out of the pool that lay between him and the entrance to the cave.

"I'm not dead," he said aloud and tried to be glad about that instead of scared. "We're not drowned."

Sport's soaked tail waved in answer. Standing on his straight legs to look down at Mickey, he looked like he was waiting to be told where to go from here.

"We're in a cave." Mickey shivered at the thought. The chill he felt inside was colder than the temperature in the eerie cave. "The undertow pulled us in here. This miserable cave probably makes the water do that."

He remembered Chuck shouting 'Dad, don't jump' and his eyes flew to the frothing opening below the sunlit surface of the river. Half of him hoped his dad would come tumbling through to the inside pool while the other half prayed that Chuck had kept him from jumping overboard.

"I guess you saved my life," he told Chuck's bright-eyed dog. "You'll probably get a classy medal and your picture in the paper. I'll catch hell, unless Mom's so glad to see me she won't make me go fishing any more."

His hand rubbed at his raw throat. "This would make a good excuse for staying home from now on. A deal like this could make a guy sick in the head."

His head felt weird, not full of water, but airy and light. He discovered that his fingers didn't feel right either. The tips were numb and his knuckles had trouble bending. His hands felt like they belonged to someone else, and he decided shakily, "Better lie still for a minute."

Sport whined and dropped down to press closely against him, sharing warmth.

"Smelly floor mop," Mickey muttered, not minding the dog's wet fur now. "I'll bet Chuck's mad as the devil at me for getting you into a mess like this. Joking my way out of this deal isn't going to be easy. There could be a dozen tunnels out of here."

His eyes had trouble focusing on the luminous dial of his waterproof watch, an early birthday present from his dad to bribe him to go camping and he realized that twenty minutes ago he had been in a rowboat on top of the river.

Now he was under it, and he told Sportin' Life, "We're going to have to wait for somebody who knows the way out of here. I'm in no shape to go hiking."

Chapter Two

Mickey stood unsteadily on a wide, rocky ledge, staring at the immense volume of water pouring into the underground prison. He told the restless Golden Retriever who scrambled up beside him, "That's gotta be the way in, not the way out. This is one of those deals that call for patience, Stinky-bear, so let's not get in an uproar, like Dad says. Let's just do the job in front of us."

His impersonation of his father wasn't up to his usual standard. He felt weak and dull-headed after his close brush with death, the memory of which was slowly fading like a dream after reality had returned. He didn't know enough about caves to be terrified or even pessimistic. All he knew was he didn't like it in here.

He told himself, "I've been in trouble before and somebody always got me out. Someone will come, Sport. They must know where that sneaky undertow leads. They'll bring lights and everything... a warm blanket, food. Listen, it would be stupid to go prowling around in pitch dark, so you just stick around too, Nosy."

Sport had wandered to a tunnel leading into blackness and his nose was raised as if he smelled something interesting he wanted to explore.

Mickey's voice was hoarse commanding Chuck's pride and joy; "Don't you take off. You can go exploring later with Chuck and Dad. They'd probably like that, but this sure isn't my kind of fun. Get back here, Dumb-bell! If you're not with me when they come for us Chuck will skin me alive. You'd like that, of course."

Sport knew Mickey wasn't his master and he only divided his attention between two gloomy-looking passageways that interested him. Then, spotting something especially fascinating wedged into a crevasse, he eagerly charged after the prize.

"Darn it, will you leave things alone?" Mickey scolded him nervously. "You could start a rockslide in here with all your barking and pulling at things that are none of your business! What's that? It looks like a jacket."

Sport let go of his treasure reluctantly when Mickey reached for it. "Someone lost a jacket overboard or --" His eyes darted fearfully over the dim cavern. A dead body might be lying nearby, with the jacket's owner as drowned as he would have been if a nervy dog hadn't made himself responsible for his master's little brother.

"It's kind of new, even if it is damp and dirty. Corduroy, I think. Either brown or dark blue, with a good warm lining. It's too big for me, but I'm glad you found this. A jacket's just what I need to keep from catching pneumonia in this disgusting dungeon."

The outside air had been a sunny seventy-seven degrees while the temperature in the cave was probably below sixty and far from dry. A damp soiled jacket big enough for his dad was better than none at all.

The minute Mickey put it on he felt better. "It's a good omen," he insisted. "Proof that luck's on our side. What else can you find? But go slow now. The floor's slippery as heck and my eyes aren't used to the dark. Listen, we'll

8

have to stay where they can see us, you know…. I sure wouldn't want to spend the whole night in here."

They circled the pool slowly, beach combing to kill time and pore over treasures the undertow had brought into the cave. Pieces of broken fishing rods were unexciting. A rusted flashlight with corroded batteries was a disappointing find, and then two bailing buckets and a rotting oar that lay beside a stiff, ancient shoe proved that all the river's discards ended up where Michael Karst Barnes found himself trapped with his brother's dog.

He mused aloud, "Everything comes in; nothing goes out." He went to look more closely at something large and light-colored that lay on a narrow ledge jutting out from a dark tunnel entrance.

He took a fast step back and his shocked breath locked in his chest. He choked, "No!" and tried to look away from the blood-curdling sight. But it hypnotized him and he stared with horror at the skeleton of a young child, drawn up to perish in a pathetic position, lying on its side to face the mouth of the cave as if hopelessly resigned to this lonely resting place.

Sour acid rose in Mickey's throat and he almost threw up. "Ohh," he panted and held a trembling hand over his eyes to shut out the sight. He sobbed, "God!" and tripped over his shoelace as he scrambled away from the awful evidence of death. He twisted his ankle and yelped, "Ow!"

A child had drowned, or waited for rescuers who never came, not even to collect the mortal remains so whoever it was could be given a proper burial. Maybe the kid had starved to death waiting for parents who still didn't know what had happened to their son, or daughter. He wouldn't look again to find out which. Boy or girl, it didn't matter now, because that child had been dead for years.

9

He began to shake with chills and he wept through chattering teeth to the sympathetic dog, "We c-can't stay here, we could wait forever! We've got to get out of here!"

But without light, how could they go anywhere?

He stormed with helpless fury; "A person would have to be stark-raving mad to go charging into a tunnel to look for a way out. Night-time could come while we were wandering around in a stupid cave and we wouldn't know it."

He hugged the heavy jacket closer around his shaking body and tried to put his hands in the pockets to warm them. They were zippered closed and his tingling fingers could feel hard objects zipped inside. Hope was born and he prayed, "God help us or we'll never get home."

Willing objects to appear, he chattered, "Flashlight, vitamins, a map." He hoped with all his might that the owner of the jacket had planned to go cave exploring instead of fishing.

"A pocketknife!" His fingers identified it before his eyes could verify the miracle. "That's really practical." He was thankful without knowing how useful a pocketknife might be in getting out of a cave. "Life Savers!"

His laugh was slightly hysterical identifying two packages of the candy. "Sugar's energy," he told Sport, "and I'll save them until I get really hungry. I'll just have one now to take the foul taste of the river out of my mouth."

The Life Saver turned out to be his favorite flavor, cherry. Another good omen. The other pocket held only a small metal cylinder, but when he got it open he let out an excited yip. "Matches! A box of waterproof matches! Light, Sport, the way out! We're saved!"

He struck a match and the bright flame warmed his spirits. "Look at that! Now we'll be able to find our way through a tunnel to the outside!"

He held the windproof flame high and turned to look around the prison that would not be Michael Barnes' final resting-place. Glimpsing again the remains of the child who couldn't have been more than six or seven years old, he cleared his aching throat and forced his breathing to steady.

"All we have to do --" his voice barely rose above a whisper -- "is decide which of those tunnels will get us out the fastest. A whole box of waterproof matches has got to be enough. Because they wouldn't be here with this nice warm jacket unless we were meant to get out. Sure, this whole deal was just to teach me a lesson. Which I will never forget! Listen, God, I promise. From now on I'm gonna learn everything I need to know."

***

A long while later he said angrily, "You're crazy, Sport! That way goes down, and we have to go up."

The stubborn Golden Retriever was determined to choose a rocky route that apparently led nowhere, and Mickey ordered, "We're taking the widest possible way out of here, a nice dry climb with lots of fresh air. Come on."

But the way he chose came to a dead-end three matches later. The tunnel hollowed out into a shrinking cavern that would soon cease to be because the stalactites and stalagmites were starting to grow together.

The match flickered out and burned Mickey's fingers. He dropped it and swore, "Hell," then defended profanity even his mother would have forgiven. "Well, I'll never get any closer to hell than this."

He made himself retrace his steps with only enough light to check the route back. His matches would run out fast at this rate, and there might come a time when he would need them more than now. Peering at his watch, he saw that it was ten minutes to four. The ticking watch and luminous dial seemed to be the only proof of reality in this living nightmare.

The second escape route he chose, forcing a sullen Sport to go ahead of him, proved too low on oxygen to support a flame. Mickey remembered Chuck saying about cave exploring; *'If a match won't burn freely, the air won't support a person for long.'*

He realized that was another reason to conserve his matches, so he could test a passageway's supply of air. Returning to their starting point, he told the four-year-old dog Chuck had trained, "It's your turn to pick a tunnel, Fuzzy-brains, but remember I can change my mind if I don't like your choice."

Sport's tunnel went down for a while, then sharply up and around a turn. He was scampering eagerly ahead when Mickey's nostrils detected a sickening odor.

He ordered, "Come back, Sport, that's not fresh air! Besides I've gotta sit down for a minute." As desperately as he wanted out, he kept getting winded. He was panting as he complained, "I told you I wasn't in any shape for this. After all, I almost drowned, you know."

Mickey knew he was a failure as a hiker. An hour's push on a level path would make him ready to quit for the day, and he muttered, "Baby-fat," nursing the insult that still stung. "No wonder your beloved master is skinny as a worm. Chuck's always running around like Superman to prove what a big, tough man he is."

Sport gave a happy bark at the mention of Chuck's name and Mickey snarled, "Don't do that!" A vibrating rock had loosened behind them and a few more followed its path as he whispered hoarsely, "We might have to go back that way, so just be quiet, you hear? Be quiet."

He said as they sat in total darkness, "Now I can tell somebody what it would be like to be blind." He closed his eyes, preferring the anonymous darkness behind his eyelids to that of the horrible cave and had another Life Saver to calm his stomach. Then he warned Chuck's dog, "The next tunnel better be it, Bird-brain, because our matches are running out. I'm gonna save one, no matter what. Just in case, for luck." A souvenir of this nightmare to remind him of his promise to learn everything he needed to know.

Close beside him, Sport's body trembled in an echo of his fear, and Mickey asked, "Are you scared?"

Did dogs ever think about dying? He scolded the Golden Retriever, "Listen, Feather-head, don't lose your nerve on me, because I'm counting on you to go for help as soon as we get out of here. My legs are about to give out."

He had to go to the bathroom before he did anything else; that was for sure. After that small problem was out of the way he said, "We'll go to the turn and then light a match, because we already know what's that far ahead. Come this way, Sport, it smells too awful that way."

The dog barked and refused to retrace his steps. Mickey hissed, "Be still! Do you want to get us permanently sealed in?"

Sport tugged at Mickey's pant leg and growled.

"Oh, for cryin' out loud! All right, if you're so sure! But you'd better know what you're doing, Dog. Because if you aren't dead-right this time, it's your funeral."

The minute the words were out he regretted them. Chuck was always saying that dogs had instincts people had lost, and Mickey prayed that he was right. Chuck was smart, but he made mistakes sometimes. Dad respected Chuck, and Mom agreed that her oldest son was just about perfect, but she secretly liked Mickey best. He was her baby, that was why, and she was letting him grow up his own way in his own time. She had told him, "The first child is always a guinea pig, while the second is to be enjoyed."

Thinking about his mom, Mickey fumbled for the match container and dropped it.

"Dammit!" He dropped to his knees on the floor of the tunnel to feel around for it. "Yichh!" His fingers slipped in

13

gooey, smelly residue and his teeth ground. "I hate this place! I'm swear, I'm never going on another vacation as long as I live!"

As long as I live echoed back to him over and over. A paralyzing fear made his stomach cramp and he whined, "Sport? Where are you, boy? Don't bark, just get back here and help me find the matches."

Exhausted from the search when he finally found them, he snarled at the Golden Retriever, "Your instinct is all in your tail, Stupid! Matches, see? Here's what I was telling you to find with your useless nose! Boy, am I going to have a few things to say about you to your master when we get back to camp! Don't rush me, all right?"

Sport was nudging impatiently at him and Mickey said, "Your high-class instinct only picks the worst stinks to follow!" But if he turned back now they might have to spend the night in the cave. Dinnertime was approaching and he said bitterly, "I hope they didn't catch a single fish."

He realized then that Chuck and his dad wouldn't have kept fishing after he fell overboard. He mused, "Wow, I bet they've even called the Ranger Station. Mom's probably having a fit n'a half. I bet she's sorry now that she made me go fishing." Tears stung his eyes at the thought of what his family was going through, not knowing that he was still alive down here. "Poor old Dad, he probably feels awful. Maybe everybody thinks I drowned.

"Sport, slow down!" he wept. "I can't keep up. We're going to run out of matches!" The match he held flickered out as if to prove it and he panted through his tears, "Give me a minute, please."

Sport whimpered nearby and came back to him. Mickey's trembling chin squared and he commanded himself, "No more thinking about Mom and Dad until we get out. Or even Chuck…" who was probably searching every inch of the woods by the lake to try and find them.

Remembering what a good buddy Chuck had been when he was sick with the mumps last year, Mickey growled, "Chuck would say 'crying won't get you anywhere, Dumb-bell' and he's right."

He sniffed back his tears and wiped the wetness from his cheeks to say, "Okay, Sport, on to the manure patch. You seem to know where you're going."

***

An hour later, with only four matches left, Mickey was ready to scream with frustration when he saw light ahead.

"Is it --" he peered ahead, holding his breath and wasn't sure. "Is that an opening? Yeah, but it's almost dark. Jeez, we've been in here for hours!" His watch told him that it was almost seven o'clock. "But you found it, boy, you were right! Good dog! Shh, don't bark; be quiet. It's not much further now, not more than a quarter of a mile."

Mickey wanted to run, but he knew better. "God almighty, what's that ghastly smell? A hot shower is what we're going to need most when we get out of here." A hot shower was going to feel like heaven.

Something alive fluttered by his face, then another something, a flying creature. "Uhh!" he cowered against the wall to gasp, "Bats!"

Sport's body, leaning heavily against him, shook in terror and Mickey shuddered saying, "Nightmare, I'm going to dream about this for a month."

They pressed on more cautiously. The outside light faded and Mickey lit another match. The thought that the torture would soon be over kept him going. People would be overjoyed to see him alive and safe. He would be treated like a hero at Pinecrest Camp and given hot chocolate and a warm bedroll to stay wrapped in for as long as he wanted. Maybe he could spend the whole vacation reading comic books while he was getting well.

15

They reached the source of the dusky light and he stopped in horror.

The walls of the cave fell away into a deep pit that stretched further than he could see. Bats by the hundreds clung to the rocky walls, and several of the spine-chilling creatures flew across the chasm to a moonlit entrance that was still a quarter of a mile away, and impossible to reach.

Words failed Mickey and he wanted to kick Chuck's dog into the stinking bat chasm. His furious hand fastened on a loose rock and he heaved it into the black pit. The rotten smelling stuff he was wading through was bat droppings, and he knew he would remember the sickening odor for the rest of his life.

An endless moment later he heard the rock bounce off of something far below, then echo as if hitting the walls again and again. The pit had a bottom, a long way down, and Mickey ranted, "That's the last time I'll ever trust you! I used up all my matches on your miserable instinct! Oh sure, fresh air!" His voice shook with fury. "Right there! But no way to get there, and I'm supposed to spend the night with bats!"

As if reacting to his anger, the bats began to swarm, following a wide-circling pattern that led to the freedom outside. They rose in a huge black body like smoke from a forest fire, their wings battering the air with a deafening roar. Mickey screamed and hit at them with his hands, fighting off bats until he lost his balance and fell, clutching at the floor in terror that he was falling into the chasm.

He made a frantic grab for Sport and hung on for dear life as he wept in despair, "Wings, that's the only way we'll ever get out of here. Oh, Sport, you're as stupid as me."

Chapter Three

It would have been suicidal to stay where they were, but to move through total darkness could lead to disaster. Horribly aware of that, Mickey's steps were slow and faltering. As soon as the bat guano thinned enough so he could sit down without wallowing in filth he sat huddled close to Sportin' Life and they rested.

Exhaustion made him fall asleep. Whenever Mickey roused he reached for the comfort of a Life Saver, and before he had slept long enough to be able to go on he had eaten all of them. Being able to rest, his layer of baby fat, and swallowing more than his fill of the river water made it possible to keep going. Sportin' Life's living presence kept him from being alone.

He pushed blindly forward, knowing that a chasm could open up without warning or a rockslide could bury them. Once he thought he heard rushing water and he wondered if a cloudburst would make the cave system become a raging torrent. Putting one foot in front of the other to shift his weight in slow motion, he muttered, "People go insane in caves."

The idea wasn't as frightening as it should have been. He reasoned that if he went crazy he wouldn't be scared or hungry or in pain. He recalled the sensation of drowning and thinking death wasn't so terrible after all. Someone had been there; something was waiting.

He heard his breathing echoing in the cave and lit a match to look around. They had come to a large white cavern with a high ceiling, and even in his shattered state he could see that the place was beautiful. It was like a king's throne room with an elevated chair at one end and a miniature waterfall at the other. A rippling stream ran through the center of the glistening cavern and the fish swimming in the stream were pure white.

Mickey bent down to look closely at them and saw that they had no eyes! As he stared in amazement, his last match flickered out, the one he had planned to save.

He sighed with regret and cupped his hands to take a drink from the stream; then he quickly spit it out. The water tasted awful! Maybe it was poisonous, but he had already swallowed some and it was too late to put it back.

Sport's head ducked into the water to grab one of the blind fish in his mouth. He tore at the meat hungrily and Mickey swallowed hot saliva, sickened by the sound. He knew he should eat some to keep up his strength. As if reading his mind, Sport waited politely, standing over the half-devoured fish the same way he would stand by a rabbit Chuck had shot.

Mickey touched the slick fish with his finger and shuddered. He pulled off a tiny sliver, took a deep breath and forced himself to swallow it whole. He gagged on it and threw up in the stream.

Sport finished his meal, carefully licking the skeleton clean; then he went into a corner to lift his leg. When he came back Mickey warned him, "If we don't get out of here by tonight we're both goners. Of course, you could probably live on snakes."

He wished he hadn't thought of snakes. It didn't do any good to tell himself not to think scary thoughts. Trying to erase them from his mind only made them get louder.

Sport checked out five exits from the King's Throne Room and chose a large, dry tunnel where the air smelled almost fresh. As they started off Mickey saw that the face on his watch wasn't luminous any more. The absence of light had made time stop for them.

A long while later the tunnel turned and went sharply downhill. Some loose rocks slid underneath Mickey's feet and he pitched forward, knocking Sport to one side. He screamed as he fell, desperately clutching at rocks to try and stop his fall, and the accumulating vibrations triggered a rockslide. A gigantic roar filled the cave and the narrow passageway behind them was sealed.

Dust filled the air and the echoes of Mickey's racking cough made him afraid that the rockslide would start again. It was terribly quiet in the cave and he whispered, "Sport?"

A suffocating silence answered him.

"Sportin' Life?" Daring to raise his voice, he begged, "Oh, please don't be caught under the rocks. I don't want to die here alone."

The Golden Retriever whimpered softly from several feet away.

"Where are you, boy?" Mickey groped his way toward the living sound. "Tell me quietly, Sport."

The panting dog lay at the outer edge of the rubble, shaking with fear. Mickey's breath escaped with relief and he sympathized, "Scared, I know. Listen, I'm sorry I cussed you out last night at Bat Chasm. Are you okay?"

Sport's tongue licked his hurt hand and Mickey sighed; "Blood... It's a good thing Dad made me get a tetanus booster. Lie still, there's no rush. There's either a way out or there isn't, and trying to hurry could wipe us out."

After a short rest they went on, a few feet at a time. At an obvious junction where they had to choose between several paths Sport couldn't make up his mind and Mickey said wearily, "It's anyone's guess. I'll take the blame this time. My instincts could get as lucky as yours."

***

Hours later, a spear of sunlight beckoned from around a turn. Mickey thought he was dreaming or that he had gone crazy. The sunlight could be an optical illusion, like a pool of water on the desert, and he repeated, "Oh let it be, let it be..." He warned the eager dog, "Don't run, Sport. God, don't let us fall into a trap now."

A minute later he said joyously, "That's it, we're out!"

The sunlight was wonderfully real and he chattered with relief, "Even if we're lost in the woods -- even if we have to spend the whole night out there and part of tomorrow, I won't complain. It's honest daylight, sunlight! Blue sky... oh, it's so beautiful!"

They had come to an open space and Mickey was nearly blinded by the brightness. There were trees and fluffy white clouds overhead, singing birds and light!

Then he moaned, "Ohh," and fell to his knees in anguish. Forty feet up, narrowing as it rose, the cave opening had water-smoothed walls that were impossible to climb.

He yelled furiously, "No, let me out! Help! Dammit all, let us out!"

His clenched fist slammed against the rock wall of the cave and his burning eyes raked this new prison where sunlight mocked their predicament. Twittering birds flew freely in and out and Mickey roared at the sky overhead, "Give me wings!"

The final insult was a rotted rope that hung on the shadowed north wall of the cave opening. The rope dangled out of reach ten feet above Mickey's head and his roar became a shattered wail. "Why are you doing this to me?"

He covered his face with his grimy, bloody hands to shut out the tormenting light. Then his hands dropped to his sides and he stared with disbelief at some crooked writing on the wall.

"What?" Stumbling closer to read the sign, it occurred to him that he had died. Maybe being lost in the cave was a timeless dream between drowning and whatever came next.

A bony gray skeleton lay beneath the words on the wall. The remains staring up at the blue sky could have been Mickey Barnes years from now, but the name he read through a brownish blur made no sense at all.

Harold Simpson. October 9, 1932.

"Harold Simpson?" Mickey's bewildered eyes drifted down to Simpson's forty-seven year old remains. Both of the skeleton's legs were broken.

Looking back at the rotted rope he couldn't have climbed even if it would support his weight, Mickey told the skeleton solemnly, "You were even stupider than I was, Mr. Simpson. You wanted to come down here."

Sport came to drop a stiff canvas bag at Mickey's feet. Then he went to flop down as far as possible from Harold Simpson's remains and lick at his cracked, sore feet.

The faded initials on the bag were H.R.S. and as Mickey opened it he couldn't help asking bitterly, "More matches? Something else to make us go on? Ah yes, *candles*, now that our matches are all gone." He hadn't saved a single one for a souvenir.

He was tempted to throw Harold Simpson's tallow candles at the rock wall in a fit of temper, but he dropped the bag instead to say, "All right, God. You win. I give up. I am *not* going back in that hell hole, you hear?"

He took a deep breath and shouted at heaven, "I'm staying in the fresh air, where I can see the sky and the trees, and scream myself crazy in case someone up there can hear me! Help!"

His voice cracked, his throat burned, and he began to cough as if he would never stop. Sport's watery eyes closed at the painful sound and he panted in soft, shallow breaths.

Mickey went to sit beside the despondent dog and comfort him. "Never mind, Sport. I'm not crazy."

Looking at the blood on his hands, an idea was born. His bloody finger traced June 25, 1979 on the rock wall, and then he slowly squeezed out enough blood to print MICHAEL K. BARNES.

Finishing the sign, he rested his head on the Golden Retriever's warm body and made an effort to sound sane. "You know, Sport, there are worse places to be lost. Like Bat Chasm, or the White Throne Room with the blind fish, or the tunnel that caved in... This is the only place where anyone could see or hear us. I'm never going back in the cave. Nothing can make me die there."

The numbness in his fingers crept to his elbows as he prayed with all his heart, "If no one's going to come and find us, don't let us wake up here. Be kind, God, everyone says you're kind."

Doubt crept in then and he muttered, "I'll bet Harold Simpson had an opinion about that."

***

He was in the den arguing with Chuck about which TV show to watch when his mother called, "Supper's ready, boys," and he woke up with a start.

The full moon was bright in the clear night sky. A thousand crickets in the woods above cheerily chirped about their freedom, and Sport was gone.

More alone than he had ever been in his life, Mickey sobbed, "God, no!" An animal howled close by and he realized that it was him. Then he heard Sport barking in the

22

distance and thought the dog was telling him that he had found a way out and was going for help.

Sport barked loudly in Mickey's ear and he gasped, "Oh! I thought you'd gone!" He hugged the Retriever with relief; then he pulled back in fear.

Sport had changed. His eyes looked mean and Mickey asked uncertainly, "What's wrong, boy?"

Sport growled menacingly.

"Don't you know me?" Mickey worried. "Come on, take it easy, lie down." He patted the ground beside him and tried not to look scared.

Sport's lips drew back in a snarl. His teeth bared and he growled again.

Mickey stumbled to his feet and his voice shook telling Chuck's dog, "Settle down, will you?" His hand motioned as he commanded, "Sit! Mind me!"

The Golden Retriever was backing him toward a small black tunnel and Mickey choked, "No! I'm not going in there!" He fought hysteria telling the dog, "You can go if -- Sport, stop it! I can't stand it if you go crazy."

His voice broke as he begged, "I want to stay where I can see out. Go on; get out if you can, just don't hurt me!"

He was being forced into a smaller tunnel than the one they had come through. There was barely room to crawl on his hands and knees and he yelled, "Leave me alone!"

Sport was biting at his feet. His teeth were bared, snarling a warning, and then his mouth snapped inches from Mickey's face. Unable to escape from this new terror, the black cave turned to gray, and then there was nothing.

***

When Mickey regained consciousness a dim, greenish light illuminated the tiny passageway where his body had gotten wedged into the rocks. Now Sport was lying quietly beside him as if his vicious attack had been a bad dream.

23

Pain throbbed in the ankle that had gotten twisted again and Mickey couldn't believe the sickly green color of his hands. He whimpered, "I can't hear the birds here. I want to go back to the sunlight and the blue sky."

The stubborn dog began to nose him toward the quiet green mist and he pleaded, "I'm afraid of that! Can't I even die where I want?"

Sport licked at Mickey's tear-streaked face; then he growled a stern warning to make him keep moving.

"We're going insane." Mickey closed his eyes tightly, willing the nightmare to end even if it killed him. "I just want it over with."

Sport's teeth pulled at the thick fabric of the loose jacket, ordering Mickey to move on!

"I don't have to do what you say!" Mickey kicked at him. "You're not even my dog."

Sport barked sharply and Mickey whispered, "Be quiet!" terrified that another cave-in would bury them alive.

Sport started to bark as if he would never stop.

"I'm going, I'm going!" Mickey crawled toward the misty green light and chattered, "It doesn't matter now. We won't be here much longer. I'll die, and a kind man will be waiting where it's warm and light."

The tunnel abruptly ended where it dropped into a green-gold pool far below. Pine trees were visible through a narrow slit between the top of the opening and the water's surface. Bright sunlight was shining through the small exit where the current flowed out, but the pool looked as deep as Bat Chasm. Mickey could see a few giant fish swimming in the clear green water, and Sport's bark sounded like he was commanding 'Jump!'

Mickey wailed, "I can't swim! You know that!"

Sport crouched behind him to give him a shove and Mickey snarled, "You go!" He pushed at the Golden Retriever with all his remaining strength.

24

They wrestled on the slippery ledge and the dog either fell or jumped into the water. He paddled frantically back toward Mickey, his worried eyes pleading with him to swim to freedom. The strong current pulled Sport slowly toward the sunlit opening, and then swiftly until he disappeared from sight.

Mickey slumped against the wet wall of the cave and he knew that Sport would never be able to come back. A moment later he heard the dog barking excitedly and he mumbled, "He's out..."

He stared down at the water and whispered, "Jump!"

He began to perspire in rivulets that ran down his cheeks like tears and he prayed without words, listening to Sportin' Life barking to celebrate his freedom.

He told himself, "It's the only way out, and if I'm going to die of thirst anyway it won't matter if -- ayeei!"

A thick, silky snake had wrapped itself around his arm. The horrified scream rising in his throat was choked off as he fell backwards into the chilling water below.

Chapter Four

*'Swimming is the most natural thing in the world,
Mick, why do you always make everything so hard?'*
Chuck's voice, talking inside of Mickey's head, made
him stop fighting the water and flow with the current. He
held his breath and pulled hard toward the light. He was
willing to be welcomed back into eternity, but not while
there was life left in him. Sport was free and it wasn't fair
that a mad dog be allowed to survive while his partner got
snuffed out like a match.

Sunlight blinded him as his soaked tennis shoes
touched soft, muddy ground. He found that he could stand
up in three feet of fast-moving water and then he saw that
he was being dragged toward nothingness -- blue sky, white
clouds and a sheer drop into mid-air.

Suddenly Sport was beside him, leading the way to
safety. Mickey heard the thundering roar and realized that
they were being pulled toward an immense waterfall!

Grabbing a handful of Sport's thick fur, he stumbled
toward the shore with his left hand beating at the water. Big
rocks blocked his path and as the water became shallower
he fell, pulling at handfuls of grass to drag himself up onto
solid ground.

Breathing in sweet, fresh air, the gulping sobs that shook him came from a vast and reverent relief. The soil beneath him was wet but warm and the growth was miraculously green. Caressing the good-smelling earth he had never loved enough, he wept, "Thanks, oh thanks!"

Sport licked at his salty tears and Mickey said gratefully, "You're all right. You're not crazy, I was."

He satisfied his thirst before he crawled away from the water that had been both enemy and friend. Miracle Falls had gotten its name because of its mysterious appearance out of nowhere and Mickey murmured, "Nowhere," finding that a perfect description of the cave system where they had been trapped for god-knows how long.

Surprised to see how far they were from Pinecrest Camp, he rolled onto his back to let the sunlight warm his face. Even with his eyes closed against the brightness he could see more light than there had been in the cave, and he whispered, "I never knew the sun was so bright."

His breathing steadied as exhaustion replaced relief. He wanted to offer a prayer of thanks, but he fell asleep before he could find any words that were good enough.

***

Mickey woke to find that it was afternoon. Looking around with clearer eyes, he discovered that the swift current from the misty green pool was the smaller of two rivers emerging from the cave system. The larger river was rushing over the falls with such force that no one could have struggled against it to wade ashore. The stream that had aided their escape apparently joined the main river after making a sharp turn in the rocks.

He and Sport were on a small triangle of land between two rivers that couldn't be crossed. Mickey viewed this new dilemma with astonishment and his words were drowned out by the roar of the falls.

"I'd say impossible if I hadn't been wrong about that for about three days."

He shaded his eyes with his hand as he turned to look for an escape route. Rejecting a large cave opening that looked like it would be easy to reach, he knew that a tunnel through the mountain would have seemed a logical solution a week ago. Now it would take more than a mad dog to force Michael Barnes into any hole.

"Over the top?" His head shook considering the only escape. The climb appeared suicidal, not just hazardous. "And who knows what's on the other side?"

His sore ankle was throbbing as he put one foot in front of the other and he told Chuck's Golden Retriever, "All I know is we won't faint if it's a dozen skeletons." The fact that they would be able to see rocks and trees, even at midnight, was enough for now.

Partway up the face of the crest he was tempted to toss away the heavy jacket, but the memory of shaking with cold in the cave made him decide to hang onto it. Sitting in the shade of an overhanging boulder, he saw a nametag sewn inside the collar. The tag was like the ones his mother had put in Chuck's clothes when he went to Scout camp two summers ago. The name was Blaine Kern and Mickey said, "God bless you, Mr. Kern," as he tied the sleeves around his waist. "I only hope we don't find you up here."

The sound of the falls was making him thirsty and he complained, "I want to see a living something besides squirrels." He rubbed at his stomach. "I'm so hungry I could almost eat a squirrel, do you know that?"

Sport was licking at his sore paws and Mickey sympathized, "Too bad you don't have tennis shoes. It's a lucky thing Mom made me buy new ones before the trip. My old tennies would have been hanging in gooey shreds by now."

His voice faded and he leaned his head against the rock as he said, "I could fasten a lifejacket easy now, my pants will barely stay up." He took up a hitch in his Indian beaded belt, the only project he had finished in Boy Scouts. The beads spelled MickE because he hadn't left enough room for the Y.

He sighed to say, "Good-bye, baby fat," knowing that Chuck would have eaten raw fish, even snake.

If Chuck had been lost in a cave he would have saved a match and been able to use Simpson's candles to find his way out. He wouldn't have yelled bloody murder while he was falling and triggered a rockslide.

Mickey mused, "I wonder if I could skin a rabbit if you caught one. I've got a knife."

He took out Blaine Kern's pocketknife to test the sharpness of the blade. The sun would go down in a few hours and he didn't feel ready to start climbing again. He didn't have the strength to make it to the top of the treacherous crest. If he got dizzy and made one false step...

He squared his jaw to say, "No, think about putting your feet in the right places."

Making himself stand up to go on while there was enough light to make the climb, he said, "Think about walking down the other side and finding people."

***

At the top of the crest a sudden weakness made his legs start to tremble. Lowering himself to the ground, Mickey shaded his eyes against the setting sun. He could see nothing to block their way, but there was no evidence of civilization either. There wasn't even a road. Miles of forest stretched before them with no water in sight.

Mickey drew his knees to his cramping stomach and admitted, "I don't know, Sport. There just doesn't seem to be a way. I need something to eat. Anything."

29

Sport lay down beside him to rest and Mickey coaxed, "You need to eat, don't you? Listen partner, whatever you catch, I'll swallow; even it if gags me."

It would kill him not to swallow it. The mouth didn't matter any more, only the stomach.

But Sport's eyes had closed and he was already asleep.

They slept until eight o'clock. Glad that the luminous dial on his watch was working again, Mickey knew it would be too dark by nine for anyone to find them. He sat up and mumbled, "Have to make a fire, get wood, keep the bears away. Rub two sticks together."

He didn't know how. "Cook a rabbit," he said and salivated helplessly. "Hunt something; Sport, go!"

Chuck's familiar hunting call echoed in his mind and he was tempted to yell *Go Sport!* Suddenly afraid the dog might not come back, he said, "You wouldn't leave me, not after everything we've been through. I know I'm only your master's little brother, but we're friends now, right?

"Listen, Sport," he confided in a rush, "I always liked you, honest. I only got mad at you sometimes because I couldn't kick Chuck. He was older -- stronger, you know? Oh well, smarter..."

He took in a breath of night air and his eyes followed the flight of a bird that might make a meal as he said, "They liked me though. I made them laugh. I saw things they missed. Like I can see -- a fire down there! It's a campfire! Someone's down there!"

"Hey!" He jumped up and yelled, "You down there!"

His voice was too hoarse to be heard for even a city block and he urged the dog as he stumbled forward, "Sport, come on! Where there's a campfire there's bound to be people and everything we need."

***

30

The campfire hadn't been smothered properly. A few embers glowed and the evidence of recent campers made Mickey feel even lonelier. A tent stake had been left in the ground and half a can of beer was lukewarm. A small plastic container sat on a log near the fire and a paper cup was full of water as if inviting him to help himself to a pill from a prescription.

Gulping down the water and then the beer, Mickey kept from screaming by telling himself that he didn't have the energy for a temper tantrum. He glared at the proof that living beings had been here a short while ago and then he had to laugh at the label on the prescription.

'Take one for nervousness, two for sleep.' He croaked, "God!" and couldn't stop laughing. Sport looked up from where he was trying to lick drops of water from the empty cup and gave an unhappy whine.

A wave of guilt made Mickey apologize, "I didn't leave any for you. Jeez, I'm stupid." He got the can of beer to empty the few drops that were left into his cupped palm.

Sport lapped up every bit of moisture between his fingers and sniffed hopefully at the can.

"Wood; we've gotta keep the fire going!" Mickey sprang up to fan it with his hands. "Paper, anything," he panted, crumbling up the cup.

He tore around gathering up anything he could find that would burn. "Kindling, pine cones," he chattered as Sport watched with interest. "Dry leaves, twigs, sandwi --" He almost threw it into the fire and his hand pulled back just in time.

"Sandwich?" He stared at a dried-out half of a cheese sandwich. "Yeah!" Even the dirt on it tasted delicious. He forgot Sport again and said almost viciously, "You can hunt, darn it! Go hunt, Sport. Go!"

His appetite had been teased by the dab of food and he searched for more leftovers as he picked up wood for the fire. He ordered the dog desperately, "Rabbit, squirrel, mongoose! I don't care what you find. Just go kill something we can cook! Go! Do you hear me? Go, Sport!"

The dog backed away from the angry command with hurt eyes. His head drooped as if he were being scolded and Mickey changed his tone to wheedle softly, "Good dog; good boy, Sport. Go hunt. Go!"

Sport sat down and scratched.

"God!" Mickey started to cuss out the dog. Then he remembered another command. "Find me a target, Sport." He made his voice sound like Chuck's. "Bring it here."

Sport stood up to look into the woods, then up at Mickey before he trotted off as if he understood.

Mickey whispered prayerfully, "Bring it here. Please."

***

"I did put out the fire, Flag, just like you said."

"Oh sure, Gary, just like you remembered to bring your pills. When I told you to leave the mess, I didn't mean you should sign your name to it. There's the roaring fire you said you put out, and there are your pills."

Words drifted through a dense fog of sleep and became part of a meaningless dream. Mickey had taken a pill for nervousness while he was praying for Sport to come back, with or without food, and as soon as his hunger had been satisfied by eating half a rabbit he had fallen asleep.

Blaine Kern's jacket was zipped up with the collar turned high to keep his ears warm. He heard Sport growl and knew he should rouse himself to put another log on the fire, but he was weighed down with sleep.

"A kid, Flag! And a dog... Oh, hey, I wouldn't argue with that dog about anything if I were you."

"You're not me, Gary. Easy, boy, we're friends. We're not going to hurt your little buddy. Hey, son, wake up."

32

Mickey tried to wake up. He felt drugged or sick, like when he'd had a high fever with the mumps.

"They're sure miles from anywhere... Golly, you don't suppose that kid could be --"

"I never suppose. He looks short of fourteen."

"But he's alone, and that dog's a Retriever, isn't he? If he's wearing a blue and yellow shirt I'll bet you ten bucks."

"Under whose big jacket? Hey, buddy, wake up and tell your tough dog we're friends."

It wasn't a dream. They were real people. Mickey forced his eyelids open and bit at his tingling lips to say, "Hello?" He sat up to ask, "Are you guys rangers?"

"That's right, son. What's your name?" The man knew enough about lost kids to speak slowly and clearly.

"Mickey." Grateful tears filled his eyes. "Have you got any water?" Saying the word made him pant with thirst.

"Barnes!" The younger man named him triumphantly. "The kid who drowned on Tuesday. The radio news --"

"Shut up and bring some water," the big man scolded. "Can't you see he's two breaths away from shock?"

Sport barked sharply as he reached out to loosen Mickey's jacket and he drawled, "Speak to your hound about his manners, will you?"

Mickey said huskily, "He's my brother's dog. It's okay, Sport, they're friends." He told his rescuers, "I took a sleeping pill so I wouldn't worry about bears, you know?" A smile cracked Mickey's lips and he tasted blood as he said, "I hope you guys are for real, 'cause me and Sport are due for some luck."

"Hey, we're all in luck, Mickey Barnes." The ranger's pale blue eyes were as cool as the water in his canteen, but his voice was warm and gentle. "We're glad we found you. Let me introduce myself and my partner."

"You're Flag," Mickey pulled their names from his dream. "And he's Gary."

"Right…" Flag's smile faded and there was respect in his eyes as he said, "Man, you must be one tough little kid. Take it easy on the water or you'll lose it."

"Don't forget Sport." Mickey cupped his trembling hands so Flag could pour some water into them for Sport. "We're in this together, him and me."

Chapter Five

Gary Chasen was fascinated by Mickey's tale but found it hard to believe. He glanced at his older brother to see what Flag thought as he asked, "Is that on the level?"

Flag's expression was impossible to read and Mickey said uncertainly, "I think it's all true." He cleaned the last bit of chocolate pudding out of a plastic cup and slid down into a cozy sleeping bag as he said, "I know Bat Chasm and Simpson's Hole were real. The Green Mist Pool was real for sure, but I could have imagined the White Throne Room and the fish that didn't have any eyes."

His hand rested on Sport's warm back as he confessed, "Things got a little crazy at the last and everything seemed like a dream I was having on my way to being dead."

He had no doubt that the Chasen's tent and their jeep and food were real. Flag had warmed the water for his sponge bath so he wouldn't get pneumonia, and having someone to talk to had restored reality.

He said, "Dad says I'm kind of long on imagination," and decided not to tell his family much about the cave. Not just because he might be accused of exaggerating -- it could give them a case of the double-guilts because of how he had begged to get out of going fishing.

Gary said, "Wow, that's wild." He had hung onto every word of Mickey's story like a kid reading super-comics. "And this dog is something else. I always wanted a dog like Sportin' Life, didn't I, Flag?"

Flag said, "You always wanted a lot of things we couldn't have."

Mickey punched up the pillow under his head as he asked, "How much older are you than Gary, Mr. Chasen?" He couldn't call Flag by his first name, probably because he looked more like a father than a big brother.

Flag told him, "I was a year older than you are when my brother was born. Gary's twenty-six, so figure it out."

"Really?" Mickey's dad was the same age as Flag Chasen. He looked a lot older, probably because he worked at a desk in a post office and Flag was an outdoor man. "Neither one of you look that old."

Gary acted younger than Chuck. The expression in his innocent blue eyes was like a sixth graders and his curly red-gold hair made him look like a Christmas tree angel. Flag's dark hair was a strange contrast with his light blue eyes and no one would have guessed that they were related.

Mickey told them, "I'll be fifteen next Sunday." The best gift he could have been given was life, and he asked, "Did you call in on your two-way radio and tell the rangers at Pinecrest that we're on our way back?"

Flag replied as he put the food away, "Everything's been taken care of, so take it easy and give that swollen ankle a rest. The important thing is to do things right, not fast, isn't that right?" He looked at his brother to remind him of that and Gary nodded soberly.

Mickey agreed, "For sure. I'm just glad you came back for Gary's pills. Now my mom isn't worrying her head off and poor old Dad isn't beating the brush for me." He laughed to add, "My big brother's got more nerve than sense, and he'll probably want to go exploring in the cave. I wish an earthquake would seal it closed and dry up Miracle Falls." He didn't really. The falls were beautiful even if they came from a very ugly place.

Gary blurted, "Listen, Mickey, what did you think when you saw my name on the prescription?"

"Gary, let the boy rest," Flag ordered.

Mickey yawned and admitted, "I hardly noticed it. I wouldn't have recognized my own name about then, but the directions made me hysterical because nobody was ever more nervous. Maybe I'll have to wear sunglasses until my eyes get used to seeing light."

He thought about telling Hodge about the cave and decided that anyone who wasn't there might think the experience had been an adventure instead of a nightmare.

Sport whimpered in his sleep, then shuddered as if he were dreaming that they were still lost in the cave.

Flag drawled, "Gary could use a pair of glasses himself, but he'd probably lose them and worry me gray over where they'd been left." He sounded disgusted and then he laughed to say, "Well, I can't complain. You're safe and so are we. It's clear sailing from here on out."

***

The next night Mickey told Flag gratefully, "You were right not to take me straight back to camp. Mom would have had a fit about my scrapes and bruises, and the way I smelled would have made people sick. I sure appreciate how nice you and Gary have been to me." He suspected that Gary was missing a few marbles and it seemed best to let him win at checkers as often as he lost.

"We appreciate your presence, Mister Barnes." Flag smiled telling him, "It's rewarding to be able to save a life now and then. It balances the scale, doesn't it Gary. Incidentally, it seems that three mysterious drownings in twelve years has wiped out a favorite fishing spot for care-free vacationers. They're closing down Pinecrest Camp."

He laughed like it was a joke and Mickey asked, "Really? You mean I was the third one?"

"That's right." Gary lit a kerosene lamp. "Seven years ago some New York publisher's little girl got drowned in the same place. He wanted to close Pinecrest because they never found her body. And five years before that all they found of some hunter was a stiff dried-up boot a mile below Miracle Falls. I bet they're both rotting in that gory cave somewhere. Right, Mickey?"

"Probably..." Mickey was glad he hadn't told them about the small skeleton. The Chasen brothers didn't seem to have a lot of respect for the dead, and he couldn't help asking, "How soon will I be able to see my family?"

Gary's sparkle died and Flag said casually, "I guess you may as well know the truth, Mickey Mouse. We seem to be lost." He grinned to show that he wasn't worried about that little problem.

"Lost? You're kidding..." Mickey's fear returned and he discovered that it had never really gone away. "Rangers don't get lost."

"It's because of you, Mickey," Gary defended Flag. "There were searchers were all over the place like ants at a picnic, so we had to hightail it..."

Flag finished his dangling sentence. "To look for you. And there's no reason to panic because I've got maps and we're going to get where we want to go." His ice-blue eyes glinted, telling Mickey, "So don't get any notion of taking off by yourself. Even with that animal you set such store by, you wouldn't last a week against the bobcats and the wolves and the snakes. I'm in charge here; understand?"

"Yes sir." Mickey swallowed the knot in his throat and answered respectfully, "I won't take off."

There was a tent here, a jeep to ride in, food, and somebody to be lost with. He only had to make sure of one thing. "You did tell my parents I'm alive --"

Flag whirled on him to snap, "Dammit, they know! So don't nag at me! I've got no time for stupid questions!"

Two strides took him to the door of the tent and he threatened Gary, "If you don't learn when to keep your loose mouth shut I may stop carrying you on my back."

His tone of voice made Sport growl, and Flag warned, "If that mutt gets nasty with me, I'm gonna eat him!"

He was gone, and Mickey's sense of security had fled.

After a sickening silence Gary's shoulder gave a lame shrug and he said, "Don't pay him any mind, Mickey. Flag loses his temper all the time, but he usually gets over it in a day or two." He reached for a tranquilizer and offered, "Want one?"

"No thanks." Mickey remembered how Gary's pills had dulled his senses and something was warning him that he needed to stay alert. "Does being lost make Flag mad?"

"I don't know. Go to sleep, will you?" Gary turned peevish. "Just try to be glad we found you in time so you could live a little longer."

***

"Carry wood, fill the water canteens, wash the dishes," Mickey grumbled under his breath to Sport, making sure that Flag couldn't hear him. "What am I, a slave? The mighty King sits there writing in his royal notebook and studying maps to plan his battles, or playing darts with that lethal blade he can stick through the middle of a paper plate at forty paces. He makes me and Gary do all the work."

Sport whined as if he agreed and Mickey whispered, "He treats you like a dumb donkey, for cryin' out loud. He's no forest ranger."

39

His resentment grew as he muttered, "They could be escaped convicts, hiding out in the mountains... No," he argued with his imagination. "Just because they don't act like forest rangers doesn't mean they're outlaws. They don't act like outlaws either -- at least the ones on TV."

Gary was standing at the camp table washing dishes and he laughed to razz Mickey, "Does Sport ever talk back when you talk to him that way?"

Mickey said, "Now and then, but only when he has something to say. Then he keeps talking until I obey him."

He gave Sport a small log to carry and thought about how Flag hadn't had much to say since he lost his temper. One lost teenager's family was probably frantic, at first thinking he had drowned in the river and then learning that he and Sport had been lost again with the rangers.

Why couldn't Flag use his radio to call for help? All he ever did was listen to it with a sneaky earplug so no one else could hear what he was hearing.

Maybe that wasn't a two-way radio. Maybe Flag was lying about reporting that they had been found. Maybe he was lying about everything. Flag looked like he could kill a person as willingly as Sport killed a rabbit.

Mickey stopped gathering wood and Flag tipped his head to ask, "What's on your mind, boy?"

That was an order, not a question, and Gary blurted anxiously, "Mickey's probably tired, Flag. Maybe he's --"

"Shut up, Gary." Flag grinned at his brother and his tone was friendly. "Let the kid say what he's thinking."

"And get hit for it?" Mickey didn't dare say what he was thinking.

"You've caught me in a good mood." Flag's lazy laugh encouraged him, "Unburden yourself, Mickey Mouse."

Mickey hated being called names! Dumb-bell, Stupid, Mouse... They all added up to the same thing. *You're nothin'.* He tested Flag cautiously. "I was thinking that's

40

not a two-way radio and nobody knows I'm alive." He held his breath and felt like he was walking in darkness.

"Interesting." Flag winked at Gary. "What else?"

Gary looked like he was watching an exciting movie and Mickey moved closer to Sport to say, "I was pretending to myself that you guys were outlaws, hiding out from the police." He prayed that Flag would laugh at his foolishness, but Gary's admiring eyes made his pounding heart drop to his buttery knees.

"You do have a bright imagination." Flag leaned back in his canvas deck chair to run his thumb along the side of his hunting knife. "And why do you suppose we bothered to pick you up?"

Mickey wet his lips. "I don't know, unless --" He felt like the wings of a hundred bats were pressing him against a cold rock wall and the words wouldn't come out.

"Go on," Gary whispered. "Say the rest."

"I'm a hostage?" Mickey knew it was true. "If anyone catches up with us, you'll trade --" He took in a breath and it got stuck in his chest.

Flag laughed. "I told Gary you weren't as dumb as you looked. I could see right off that you've got brains you never used 'til now. But your trouble is you should listen to the news so when you see a guy's name on a prescription you'll know when to get the hell away from his fire instead of swallowing his pill."

"Gary Chasen?" Mickey couldn't imagine what Gary could have done to be on the news.

Gary giggled. "I knew all about you from listening to the radio, Mickey, and you never heard about me and Flag." Proud as a sixteen-year-old driving a new car, he could hardly wait to impress a friend with his misdeeds.

Mickey was sick at heart and he didn't want to know. He just wanted out, but he had to ask, "What did you do?"

Flag told him, "We put half a million bucks in cold storage, and we're going to become wealthy tourists when we get out of the mountains. Consider yourself kidnapped, daydreamer. That little detail wasn't in my plan, but it seems a fair trade. We saved your skin from the bears and you might get a chance to save ours from the pigs."

He stood up to practice throwing his knife. "I figure you're in our debt as far as a man can get, Mister Barnes. So as long as you make yourself useful and don't bug me with your adolescent homesickness we'll consider you and your hunting hound valuable assets. Do you follow me?"

Mickey could only nod like a robot and say, "Yes." Not 'yes sir' to a liar and a robber, but he had no choice but to stay with Flag Chasen and his mentally deficient brother.

He knew that might prove as dangerous as finding his way out of a cave with dead-end tunnels, bottomless chasms and deep water. The day might come when he would have to sink or swim, unless he preferred facing a snake at close range.

Flag's knife stabbed into the only pine sapling twenty feet away and he said, "In case you might be wondering, this is Sunday. Happy Birthday, Mickey Mouse."

Chapter Six

"Gary, was Flag serious when he said if we didn't catch some fish there wouldn't be any dinner tonight?" Mickey baited a hook and wiped his fingers on his jeans.

Gary scowled as he tried to untangle a snarl in his line and he answered, "Flag jokes a lot, but it's best not to laugh at him. If you look scared and say 'on the level, Flag?' he can laugh at you and he likes that best."

Mickey vowed, "I will never laugh at him. I don't think he's funny. Hold my line and I'll untangle yours for you." He wouldn't say dumb-bell because he knew what that did to a guy. "What's Flag's real name?"

Gary said, "Lawrence, I think. He told me one night how the kids in school said he acted like a bull when you waved a red flag in its face, so he yelled at them to call him Flag because he hated his name anyway."

"Was he named after his father?" Mickey couldn't picture Flag as a boy, especially one named Lawrence.

Gary said, "He never told me his father's name."

"But wasn't your father --" Mickey looked up and decided to say, "Never mind. Where did he go today?" Flag had told them he was going to scout the route ahead, but Mickey had stopped believing anything he said.

Gary snapped, "I don't know!"

43

He sounded like he was being grilled and Mickey reminded him, "Hey, I already know all about you. It won't make things any worse to tell me where Flag went."

Gary pouted. "He wouldn't tell me, because he said you'd find a way to weasel it out of me."

"Smart..." Mickey gave up. "Let's just fish."

He looked at Sport prowling along the bank and wondered how far they would get with only a water canteen, a fishing pole and a flint. Taking things from robbers wasn't stealing, but he might need a sleeping bag before they found a ranger station.

"Flag told me you're smart as a whip." Gary's expression was trusting as Mickey handed back his line. "I think he likes you."

Mickey couldn't help saying, "If he didn't like me would I be dead by now?"

He was memorizing the things he was learning about survival in the wilderness, but he probably didn't know enough to get him back to Pinecrest.

Gary said, "Heck no, Flag said finding you was the last card we needed to make a royal flush. You made it a sure thing." He smiled gratefully at his hostage.

"Wow, I'm glad to know that." Mickey's humor was as dry as it had ever been. "What I always wanted to do with my life was help somebody steal a cool half-million."

Gary giggled. "You're funny, Mickey, you oughta go on TV. Listen, you should joke more with Flag. He gets tired of me sometimes, and if you're tough as nails and smart as a whip and act real don't-give-a-damn Flag might take us both ice-skating after we get out of the mountains. Maybe you could even go to Hong Kong with--" His lips pressed together and he closed his eyes.

Mickey comforted him, "Don't worry, I'm not going to say anything about Hong Kong or ice-skating. I like roller-skating better anyway." *Wheels, not blades, were his style.*

44

"I'll never rat on you, Gary. I've got a big brother and I know how it feels to be reduced to a boneless custard."

"But you've got a father and mother, too."

Gary sounded jealous and Mickey whistled for Sport before he asked, "What happened to your parents?"

"Dead." Gary sounded like he was quoting Flag. "Never mind. They weren't no good, and my sister should have been poisoned at birth."

"How come?" Mickey saw a fish cruising Gary's line and he knew they were talking too much to catch anything.

Gary said with disgust, "She got Flag in trouble."

"How?" Mickey heard Sport barking in the distance, either answering his whistle or chasing after something.

Gary said, "She had a baby nobody wanted, and after Flag took me away we had to hide from the cops."

"Why?" Mickey was thoroughly confused.

"Because they hated us!" Gary's eyes misted with hurt. "Flag's the only one in his family who ever loved me."

Mickey knew even less about sex and hatred than he knew about outlaws, and he could only say, "I'm glad he loves somebody. It makes him almost human."

Gary put his fishing rod down to beg, "Mickey, you could make Flag love you. You've gotta try! I never had a friend of my own or a dog, and I don't want Flag to --"

His breath caught and he rubbed a shaky hand across his eyes to say dully, "It's getting hot out."

"You're saying Flag's going to kill me when I'm not useful any more." Mickey knew he should be leaving right now! Was Flag testing him by pretending to be away? Was he hiding behind a bush, listening to every word? Where the devil was Sport?

Gary yelped, "Dammit-all, I didn't say that!"

"When?" Starving to death was one thing, but murder was something else. "How? With the gun or the knife?"

Gary started to cry. "Don't ask me, Mickey, please."

45

"Tonight, tomorrow?" Mickey gripped Gary arm and the hard muscles under his fingers reminded him that Flag's brother wasn't a child, but a grown man.

He spoke quietly, pressing him for an answer. "Gary?"

Gary shook off his hand. "No, not for a long time."

"Boy, he must really like me." Mickey's laughter shook. Gary was probably innocent by reason of insanity, and someone should have arrested his brother years ago so he could go to a mental hospital. "How many people has Flag killed?"

Gary exploded. "If you keep asking me mean questions, Mickey Barnes, I won't be your friend! I'll take your dog after you're dead."

"I was only joking." Mickey forced a smile and wiped perspiration from his face. "Listen, we can be best friends. We can be blood brothers; would you like that?"

"On the level, Mickey?"

Gary sounded younger than Hodge and Mickey nodded to promise him, "On the level."

It wasn't a barefaced lie. Gary Chasen needed a friend more than anyone he had ever known, and if they became blood brothers Gary might start comparing the way Mickey treated him to the way his brother made him feel.

Five minutes later their names and the date were printed in blood on a smooth boulder that faced the stream.

Mickey warned Gary solemnly, "If either of us tells anyone about this, the secret pact will be instantly broken."

Flag would probably break Mickey's neck and cover the marker with his and Sport's blood.

"I promise." Gary stared at the blood on his finger and whispered gratefully, "Now if Flag gets killed by the dirty cops I'll still have a brother to keep me alive."

Mickey vowed, "I'll see that you get whatever you need." He prayed that Gary wouldn't be shot if their childish pact helped the police find them.

46

Gary offered eagerly, "I'll beg Flag to let you go with us. I can almost always get what I want -- unless it's bad for me, of course. Mickey, would you try to make him see you're on our side? You'd make such a great outlaw."

Mickey was stuck for an answer and he was relieved to see Sport come through the trees carrying a furry body in his mouth. He laughed, telling Gary, "There's dinner, even if we don't catch anything. Good boy, Sport!"

"Yuchh!" Gary made a face and looked away. "I hate seeing things that are dead. It reminds me of Angela."

Mickey's smile froze on his face and he couldn't help asking, "You mean Flag's sister?"

"It's a secret," Gary said stubbornly. "I'm gonna fish."

After a moment Mickey mused as if he were talking to himself, "Well, I suppose whenever someone gets away with half a million bucks, somebody has to die."

"That's exactly what Flag said!" Gary's eyes filled with wonder at a blood brother's understanding. "'Whenever somebody wins somebody else has to lose.' And it's not like we robbed normal people like you. Flag said the Wheeler Escrow Company was insured to the hilt. Nobody lost anything, Mickey, except fat fools like Marty Wheeler, with his four houses and his prize poodles who weren't half as smart as Sport."

Mickey was aware of the risky game he was playing as he baited Gary. "I'll bet that took some doing. You really pulled something, robbing an escrow company." He had thought that robbers only hit banks or convenience stores, depending on how many people they were willing to kill.

"Flag planned it all." Gary was modest. "But he said we couldn't have pulled it off unless I made Angela Wheeler want to marry me bad enough to die."

Mickey dreaded hearing the rest. "Did you like her?"

"No! She wasn't even pretty, and she was older than me. Her father told Flag we didn't have enough brains be-

47

tween the two of us to make a family. But he loved Angie like Flag loves me, and after we got engaged the old fool trusted us the way Flag said he would."

After a moment Gary added with an unhappy shrug, "Like Flag says, they're better off dead. It would have been embarrassing to have to tell all the wedding guests that we were only after their money."

That whole story had been in the newspapers and on TV and Mickey had never heard a word of it. Chuck barely listened to the news while he did his homework, but if he had seen Gary Chasen's name on a prescription he would have known enough to stay away from his campfire.

"Did you have to kill anyone else?" Mickey cleared huskiness from a throat that was threatening never to regain the piping laughter that had endeared him to his mother.

"Flag killed them, I only watched. I'm chicken."

Gary sighed with regret about his cowardice. "Flag had to shoot a nosy woman who saw us running to our car, but she didn't die. That's why we have to color our hair. She told the cops we were very light blond. She said I was handsome and Flag was big and athletic. Angela told me I was handsome. God, wouldn't you rather be called big and athletic any day of the week? Oh, look, Mickey! There's a great big fish on your line!"

Gary shouted with excitement, "Quick, pull him in! Oh boy, Flag is gonna be so proud of us for catching that fish!"

Chapter Seven

Rain fell for three days and the forest turned to a swamp. Flag had turned friendly again and Mickey was glad he wouldn't have to strike out on his own this week because the weather was so bad. He stayed in the tent most of the time, storing information about survival in the wilderness while he kept a close eye on his murderous overseer for any sign that the coolie labor was about to get worse than a tongue-lashing.

Sport's opinion of the brothers was obvious. He went to Gary willingly, but he would sit with his back turned to Flag to express his canine contempt. Flag thought that was funny, but he warned Gary that wasting his time teaching a hunting dog parlor tricks would only result in having roasted dog for supper.

Mickey could see that Flag was jealous of anyone Gary liked. That appeared to be a weak link in his armor, but he wouldn't share that important clue with anyone but Sport.

Gary and Mickey played poker to pass the time until the weather would clear enough for them to travel. Since Mickey didn't have any money Gary gambled recklessly, "A thousand dollars against your beaded belt."

Mickey laughed. "Sure, one bead of Indian wampum at a time." The belt wasn't even worth five bucks.

Flag chuckled at the boys' game as he watched from a few feet away and cleaned his gun. He seemed to have stopped worrying that his fifteen-year-old hostage would run away and he nodded to agree when Gary argued, "No, that would ruin it. I want the whole belt just like it is!"

Flag egged him on. "Your name isn't Mickey Mouse so we'd have to restring the belt to say Gary."

"Could you do that?" Gary asked eagerly. "Could it say my name, Flag?"

"You bet," Flag nodded and polished his revolver.

Mickey mentioned, "We'd have to buy a loom," and he thought about trying to get the gun. God only knew how many people had been killed with it, but if he failed, it would be his last failure on this earth. Nothing had prepared him for that kind of a contest, while Flag had had forty years of experience.

Mickey reminded Gary, "It's your deal," and wished that Sport would stop his nervous pacing and settle down.

"Could we make a loom?" Gary worried.

Flag promised, "Sure; win the stupid belt and I'll restring it for you."

Gary said, "Maybe Mickey could teach me to do that."

"Maybe..." Flag's flat tone revealed his jealousy.

***

Before it stopped raining Mickey won seven hundred and twenty-two dollars, at least on paper. Gary was pouting, but not about losing the money. He couldn't pay up anyway until they collected their loot from the robbery. He was just aching to wear Mickey's belt.

Mickey tried to explain, "But I won, Gary, fair and square. That's the way the game goes." He could have said *'Somebody wins and somebody loses'* but he was learning when to keep still.

50

Flag advised Gary, "Keep playing until you win. We can afford it, and there sure isn't anything else to do."

Flag would have paced the tent if he were a dog, and Mickey dared to say, "I'm very lucky at cards. Would you like to play me for the gun?"

He delivered his sunniest grin, following Gary's advice to make Flag like him. Nobody could make him go to Hong Kong instead of home, except at the point of a gun.

Flag laughed. "Would you kill me, Mister Barnes?"

Mickey kidded back, "Why would I want to do that? How would I learn all the things you have to teach me?"

Gary's gasp was admiring and Sport looked impressed.

Flag's head tipped and he looked sideways at Mickey. "Oh, very fast, but not very clever." A microsecond later the long knife was across Mickey's throat and Flag was asking, "How tough are you now, Mickey Mouse?"

About as tough as a banana skin with cold steel pressed to his neck.

Then Sport crouched and sprang, knocking Flag to the floor of the tent and locking the hand with the knife in his bared, snarling teeth. Flag swiftly counter-attacked, and Mickey barely had time to think about the gun before an airborne Golden Retriever was flung through the loose tent door to land on the ground outside with a sickening thud.

Flag sounded more disgusted than angry swearing, "Some day I'm going to kill that miserable animal. I ought to slit your wisecracking throat, Super-mouse. Do you know how easy that would be?"

Mickey answered humbly, "Yes, I know that."

Trying to take a murderer's gun away from him was a stupid idea that only worked in the movies. Praying that Sport's neck wasn't broken after the way his head had been jerked back, Mickey said, "I'll go have a talk with Sport in case he has any doubt."

"You do that." Flag's satisfied grin returned. "And I'll design a loom to restring that belt. I'm fairly lucky at cards myself, Mister Barnes."

The rain had turned to a mist as Mickey knelt beside the chastened dog to whisper, "Sport? Are you all right? Don't quit on me, I'll never make it home without you."

The Golden Retriever's dazed eyes looked up at him and Mickey said with relief, "Take it easy, you're okay."

Sport lurched weakly to his feet. The glazed expression left his bewildered eyes and he looked sadly at Mickey to admit total defeat at Flag's hands.

Mickey patted him to whisper, "Never mind. I haven't got his sick sense of humor figured out yet, so we can't take any chances. If either of us triggers that bull's temper we're both in for it. I hope to god you understand me, Sport, because I don't know how to make it any plainer than he just did. The thing is, we need to act with dignity, like Dad says, but not get too high-hat. We have to do whatever Flag tells us and watch for our chance to make a break for it. Boy, I'd like to see him get caught. Gary needs so badly to see Flag lose."

Flag won easily at cards; he knew ways. He was an expert bluff and he cheated with confidence.

A few days later Gary wore the coveted Scout belt and Flag was in no hurry to restring the beads. It gave him pleasure to see Gary wearing the loser's name.

The loss was hard for Mickey to swallow. At home, giving up the belt would have meant very little, but here in the wilderness, with nothing to call his own except his watch and the clothes on his back, the belt had become a symbol of his identity.

Setting up camp in a new place, Mickey's blood boiled as he watched Gary strutting around to flaunt his disregard for fair play. Flag tested a fifteen-year-olds self-control by taunting, "Where's our Sunshine Boy? No funny jokes to-day, clown-face?" He stood ready to slap Mickey down if he got impertinent.

"I'm planning them," Mickey mumbled. "You'll die laughing later." Then he started to quake inside, wishing that he had said no sir instead of pushing his luck.

But Flag said, "You'll do, Barnes." He smiled and his pale blue eyes reflected the Wyoming sky. "Come here."

Mickey realized as he walked to Flag that the hot feeling churning in his guts was hatred. It was a new feeling, much worse than being sick. Gary was standing by the jeep and his face was wincing in dread of seeing his best friend beaten, but Flag only murmured, "Don't hurt Gary's feelings. Be nice to him."

Mickey replied quietly, "I'm not mad at Gary. I don't blame him for anything." That was the honest truth. Nothing was Gary's fault.

Flag frowned and glanced at Gary. His expression softened and Mickey knew they shared the same concern for an ageless child who hadn't been right from birth. That seemed to give them a meeting ground and Mickey told Flag with a dignity that was only a little high-hat, "I don't write off a friend because his big brother leaves me cold."

If Flag smacked him for that it would hurt Gary more than it would hurt him. Gary might even help him escape.

Flag's head tipped to one side and his mouth pursed in a silent 'ooh.' Then laughter shook him and he drawled, "We're going to have to get you some new clothes, orphan. You've gotten way too big for your britches. Don't you think, Gary?"

Gary whimpered and slid down by the side of the jeep to hide his eyes.

Mickey decided to answer, "I'll wear anything you've grown out of, Mister Chasen."

Flag roared with delight and slapped him on the back to say, "Damned if you won't! I'll get it right now. I'll even throw in a leather belt." He strode to the jeep to pull his duffel bag out of the back as he said, "You'd better have some winter boots, too. Summer's almost behind us."

Mickey's heartbeat slowly returned to normal and he smiled at Sport to thank him for not overreacting.

Pale with relief, Gary straightened up to lean weakly against the jeep. As Flag's duffel bag dropped to the ground the jeep started to roll downhill. Gary had been driving and he had forgotten to set the handbrake. His belt got caught on the door handle and he shrieked in terror, "Flag! Mickey!"

It didn't occur to him to try and unfasten the belt. All he could do was yell for help. Mickey ran to him and hooked his arm over the door to let himself be dragged alongside as Flag leapt onto the back of the jeep and clawed his way to the front seat.

Releasing the tight clasp at Gary's writhing waist, Mickey rolled him away from the wheels as Flag stopped the jeep and pulled on the brake.

Gary sobbed in anguish, "Take back your damn belt! It tried to kill me!"

Mickey lay sprawled in the dirt, panting for breath. His left leg had twisted painfully beneath him, and Sport gave his face a sympathetic lick before deciding that Gary was more in need of comfort.

Flag shoved the dog roughly aside and his voice rasped ordering Mickey, "Get some water and a bedroll. Bring his tranquilizers."

"Right." Mickey limped to the jeep to pull out Gary's sleeping bag and a water canteen. He poured water into a cup and found Gary's pills in the pocket of his jacket. Flipping the lid off the plastic container with his thumb, he put two pills in Gary's mouth and cheered him up by saying,

"I'll bet if we practiced that trick a few times we could scare the daylights out of Sport. He's still shaking, see?"

Flag was the one who was coming apart at the seams. Sport was probably laughing.

Gary gulped down the pills and giggled through his tears. "You're crazy, Mickey. We nearly got killed and you didn't have to be. You could have run away and nobody would have chased you." He clutched at Flag's hand to beg, "Can Mickey be our brother now? He risked his life for me, even if we stole his beaded belt."

"Sure, Gary," Flag soothed him. "Lie still and breathe easy. Don't be afraid, everything's going to be okay."

Mickey reclaimed his belt as he suggested, "We could buy some more beads and make a belt with Gary's name. It's not like we were poor or anything. He still owes me seven hundred and twenty-two bucks from our card game."

"That's the way you figure it?" Flag shook his head at the logic of a fifteen-year-old. "So what do I get for winning a cool grand off of you?"

Mickey could see that he was still badly off-balance and his answer was chosen as carefully as he would place a bet against Flag Chasen. "You probably wouldn't want your name on a belt, so how about a leather jacket with flags showing all the countries where we've traveled?"

Before Flag could decide what to say Mickey wiped the dirt off his face and told the watchful Retriever, "Let's get unloaded partner. The sooner the tent's up and dinner's over the sooner you and I can quit for the night."

Handing Flag's bedroll to Sport by its nylon handle, he laughed telling Gary, "I think I ripped the seat out of my pants. They were sure too tight for that trick. I'm getting some new ones just in time."

Chapter Eight

As Gary slept off his traumatic reminder to set the brake on the jeep, Flag brought Mickey the first aid kit and ordered him to take care of his scraped-up leg.

He razzed, "I don't want you to get any bloodstains on your new pants. They were supposed to be Gary's for our winter in the mountains, but they shrunk when I washed them. I'd have crammed them down the salesman's throat, but we had an important appointment to keep. What the devil are you doing with that peroxide?"

Mickey said, "Applying first aid?" His mother had always treated his battle wounds and he wasn't sure how.

"Give me that stuff." Flag took the peroxide away from him to pour it directly into the raw injury. "Don't tell me a tough stunt man like you can't take a little doctoring." He grinned at the way Mickey sucked in his breath. "Smarts, huh? Well, just wait until some amateur medic digs hot lead out of your shoulder, then tell me about pain."

"You were shot?" Mickey was less shocked by that than he would have been a month ago. The only reason his voice cracked was because he was getting older.

"More than once." Flag wasn't bragging, he was simply stating a fact. He taped a couple of large gauze bandages to Mickey's leg as he said, "That was before I learned that robbery is a cold, calculating business, not an exciting impulse of the moment. Now I know that organization and follow-through are what succeed in business, Mickey Mouse. Memorize that."

His brotherly advice sounded like Chuck used to in his more patient moments and Mickey sighed to say, "Okay, but I really hate that name."

More than ready to call it a day he stretched out beside Gary, who was already snoring. He wished that Sport didn't have to be a watchdog and sleep outside. He hardly ever barked, but his low growl always woke Flag instantly. Nobody slept lighter than a murderer.

Flag baited him; "If your folks had named you Donald it could have been worse. Or would you rather be a duck than a mouse?"

Mickey asked softly, "Do you really want an answer?" A wise fish cruised the bait before stealing it off the hook

"Try me." Flag put his revolver under his pillow.

"Oh sure, say what I think and get my head blown off." Mickey's laugh was bitter. "You make conversation like you play poker. Don't you ever get bored with winning?"

"Ask me that after we've picked up our winnings," Flag drawled. "Put out the lamp."

Mickey obeyed before he tested his jailer. "When my brother called me names it seemed to me that he was short on imagination. My dad says profanity is born of an inadequate vocabulary, and it's all part of the same thing."

Flag said wryly, "You're very brave in the dark. Learn that in a cave?"

"That's just my answer to whether I'd rather be called Mickey Mouse or Donald Duck. Do I get shot for it?"

"Not tonight, Mister Barnes." Flag sounded too contented to kill anyone. "You were a good boy today."

That gave Mickey the courage to ask, "What happened to Gary? I mean, what made him like he is? Did you ever get a doctor's opinion?"

Flag said with disgust, "A specialist gave me a lot of double-talk about bloodlines, but Gary's blood is the same as mine so I figured the fool had a book for a brain. I think it's because Gary's moronic mother tried to kill him nine times before he was old enough to yell for help."

"You mean abortion?"

"Abortion, infanticide, strangling; you name it, Gary lived through it. Don't talk to me about murder, Sunny-face, because you don't know the meaning of the word."

"Probably." Mickey admitted that his knowledge of the subject was limited. He couldn't even imagine a mother who would strangle her own baby.

Flag said, "A doctor at a high-priced clinic in Chicago told me that Gary would be an imbecile if he managed to live longer than five years. A quack in Denver said he'd be a delicate moron at best, so I swiped a book from a library that told me everything I needed to know. It said 'Remove the source of the irritation and treat the lack of nourishment with extra doses of the missing ingredient.' The truth is if you give a dog enough love and attention he'll be a different animal than if you only take him for walks and feed him table scraps. Isn't that right?"

"That's right," Mickey agreed. "Sport was smart when he was a puppy, but sometimes he seems almost human."

Smarter than Gary and more human than Flag.

Flag stated, "Gary's an angel compared to my drunken father, and I'm going to see that he gets what's due an angel, no matter what it takes. Somebody's gotta make that up to him! People who punish their kids for being born deserve what they get from their kids!" His anger died as fast as it had flared up and he said flatly, "Memorize that."

58

"Okay, but I'd rather not hear what it was." Mickey didn't want to know how Flag had punished his family.

"You're fairly all-together for fifteen." Flag sounded like he resented Mickey's normality. "I bet your folks spoiled you rotten."

"If I'd been any more spoiled I wouldn't have lived for an hour." An unexpected wave of homesickness threatened to make Mickey cry and lose the ground he had gained.

Flag asked, "What kept you going, Mick?"

"I'm not sure. I haven't thought about it much." The cave was best forgotten. "I guess I'd rather die on the move than sit down and think about it." He had been ready to quit in Simpson's Hole, and now he was sure that Sport had pretended to go mad to make him swim out of the cave.

Flag said fervently, "You and me both. The only name nobody will ever call me or Gary is 'poor bastard.' Gary will be rich, and as respected as I can make him."

Mickey wasn't sure how to answer that, and after a minute Flag said, "You think I'm immoral, don't you?"

Immoral was the understatement of the century and Mickey thought before he said, "Well, my dad is President of the KC Optimist Club and I went to Sunday school every week. I had a public school education, so I can't help being the way I am any more than Gary can." He wanted to stop talking now and go to sleep.

"And I guess you'll never change," Flag said sadly.

"Hey," Mickey woke up fast and argued, "I'm changing every day. Three months ago I couldn't fasten the belt on a lifejacket. Today I could do that while I was hanging onto a moving car. Maybe I won't go to church when I get home. Maybe I'll find a way to get out of going to school."

Living tomorrow and the day after that was all that mattered, and there was no guarantee of that unless he kept thinking every second of every day. He added recklessly, "What the hell; maybe I won't bother to go home at all."

59

It was a deliberate lie that came off well, and he held his breath until Flag agreed, "Maybe you won't. Get some sleep, Barney. Tomorrow's going to be longer and harder than today, and that's no joke."

Mickey let out his breath and said, "I'll be ready."

Barney was a much better name than Mickey Mouse, or even Mister Barnes, the way Flag's mouth could twist it. The subtle promotion offered as much hope as a waterproof box of matches.

***

The journey to the campsite where Flag planned to hole up for a week turned out to be tougher than he had warned. The jeep had to be pushed through thick foliage, and the road they made cut back a few times. They had to hide the deep ruts where the wheels cut into soft soil, and by the time Flag was satisfied with their efforts only a bloodhound could have trailed them.

Mickey's injured leg was hurting but Gary seemed to have forgotten about his bruises. He sang as he brushed dirt over tire tracks as if he were painting a work of art. Sport seemed to have accepted the necessity to get along with Flag and he obeyed anyone who gave him an order.

At last they pitched the tent at the base of a huge rock where tall trees circled a small open area. Flag gave his approval of Mickey's campfire by saying, "Okay, Barney," and Gary whispered, "You're *in*, I just know it!"

Flag cooked the evening meal and helped them wash the dishes instead of issuing orders from his canvas chair as he usually did. Then they sat around a nearly smokeless campfire to let their meal settle before going to bed.

Sitting there feeling warm and sleepy, Mickey realized with surprise that he felt good. For the first time in months he was relaxed, mostly because he had stopped being afraid. He couldn't help enjoying his false contentment as he told Sport, "Maybe I'll sleep outside with you, Mop."

He brushed the dog's hair the wrong way and Sport put his paws on Mickey's chest to invite him to play. Mickey groaned, "Don't you ever get tired? Help, stop, I give up!"

"Come and play with me, Sport," Gary urged, patting his chest. "I'll wrestle with you. I'm not that tired."

Flag laughed to say, "Ah, youth. Where did you go?"

That was the first time Mickey had heard him admit to being tired and he said, "Don't tell me we wore you out."

Flag drawled, "I can still hold my own, Barney. Try anything and you'll see."

Mickey yawned to admit, "I can barely drag myself to bed and it's not even dark yet. Is it okay with you if I hang out with Sport tonight?"

Flag agreed, "If you think you'll be warm enough."

He appeared to have stopped worrying about his hostage trying to escape, and as Mickey went to the tent to get his bedroll he knew he might never get a better chance to make a break for it. His backpack contained everything he would need to survive for a few days, and as he slid it closer to the door of the tent he knew that the nearest town could be a hundred miles away. But tracking anyone in the dense woods on a moonless night would be almost impossible and Flag had admitted to being tired.

The biggest problem was his own fatigue, and Mickey decided that if he slept until daybreak without waking up it would be a sign that he wouldn't have gotten very far.

He was surprised to hear Sport give an excited bark that sounded more like a greeting than a warning. Then Flag called, "Hello there! I thought we were the only people who were crazy enough to be up this far." His voice lowered murmuring to Gary, "Offer the ranger some coffee and watch your step."

A forest ranger! Mickey clutched his sleeping bag to him and his heart started to race with hope. Every ranger within a hundred miles must have seen pictures of him and Sport, and he envisioned a posse hiding in the woods, ready to strike at a moment's notice. But if he yelled for help that nervy ranger wouldn't last for five minutes.

The ranger's voice was pleasant telling Flag casually, "That looks like a fine dog. I hope you're not hunting. You've probably found out that this isn't the best fishing territory. Our wildlife can be downright unfriendly."

"We're prepared for that." Flag's tone held the smiling warmth Mickey had learned to distrust. "I'm Tom Morgan and this is my nephew, Mark."

"Hi." Gary sounded like a grown-up, imitating Flag. "Would you like some coffee?"

"I'd appreciate that." The ranger told them, "I spotted your campfire and came to caution you about bobcats. Be sure not to leave the dog tied up or do anything to invite them to your camp. I'm Blaine Kern. Are there just the two of you, Mr. Morgan?"

Mickey shot from the tent with his bedroll under his arm and said breathlessly, "Three, unless you count dogs."

It was destiny! Blaine Kern's jacket had given him his first ray of hope, and there was probably a box of water-proof matches in his pocket right now. He looked like a real woodsman wearing a fur hat and carrying a rifle. Blaine was taller than Flag and he had the solid look of morality.

Flag's grin was confident, introducing Mickey. "My other nephew, Matthew, and his dog Mortimer. The trick is to tell Mort it's not hunting season, but Matthew keeps him pretty well under control."

"He looks smart enough." Blaine smiled at Mickey and knelt to offer his hand to Sport in the way of an animal lover who knows how to approach a dog.

Sport sniffed at Blaine's hand and sat down to offer his paw to a new friend as Chuck had taught him.

"How do you do, Mort." Blaine laughed and shook his paw. "I wish my kids were as well-behaved as you. But of course they're only three and a half years old, so manners aren't their priority. Twins, a real handful for their mom."

He sat on a log to drink his coffee as he commented, "You must be veteran mountaineers to brave this natural wilderness. Did you plan to sleep outside, Matthew?"

His expression seemed to find Mickey too young for such a rigorous vacation and the way he said the phony name sounded like he doubted it. Ordinary campers didn't cover their tracks or build smokeless campfires that couldn't be seen from a quarter of a mile away.

Mickey said, "Me and Mort bunk together whenever we can." He delivered the sunny grin that dominated all the family photos to add, "You could say we're inseparable."

Flag drawled, "One of 'em starts a sentence and the other one finishes it." He had never looked less like a murderer than he did telling Mickey, "Your pet mop better sleep in the tent from now on. Just tell him not to snore."

Mickey said, "Okay," and took his bedroll back to the tent. Looking for an excuse to wear the brown corduroy jacket that was still too big for him, he offered as he emerged, "Should I get some more firewood, Uncle Tom?"

Flag agreed, "That's a good idea, but stay close."

"I will. Come on, Mort." Mickey whistled for Sport and got ready to run for his life when the shooting started. He prayed that Blaine wouldn't challenge Flag, because the deadly knife and gun were never out of reach.

Sport decided to show off instead of responding to Mickey's whistle. Trotting to Gary he rolled over playfully.

Gary said, "Good boy, roll over! Now sit up and beg."

He started to put Sport through his whole bag of doggy tricks and all Mickey could do was gather kindling and pray that the Golden Retriever knew what he was doing.

Sport was acting like he was in a circus, and finally Flag put a stop to Gary's fun by standing up to say, "Thanks for stopping by, Blaine. I wouldn't have your job on a bet. I think everyone should learn how to survive in the wilderness, considering the shaky state of the world, but I wouldn't choose to live here all year round."

Blaine replied, "I manage to divide my time between the forest and my other home. Can your dog fetch?"

Gary bragged, "Smort can do anything. Bring the ranger a present, Mort." He looked around, trying to decide what it should be, and clever Sport ran to get the dishrag that was the last remnant of Mickey's blue and yellow shirt.

"Just what I need, a damp dish rag." Blaine accepted it gravely and straightened up to say, "Take it easy, Morgans. I suppose you have flares to send up if you need help."

Flag replied, "We're equipped for every emergency."

Mickey put down the kindling and unzipped the corduroy jacket to tuck in the shirt Flag had given him. His name on the beaded belt was in plain sight as he said, "Glad to have met you, Mister Kern."

Blaine smiled to say, "You too, Matthew." It sounded like a promise as he added, "Be seeing you." He cautioned Flag as he picked up his rifle and backed toward the edge of the trees, "Don't take any chances now."

Mickey felt sure that a posse of cops was out there. Blaine had only stayed long enough to drink his coffee and there was nothing normal about that whole scene.

"We'll be fine, thanks." Flag told Gary, "Put the cooking stuff away and make sure you bury the garbage."

Gary repeated, "The garbage -- all right, Uncle Tom." He stumbled a little hurrying to the tent and Flag draped an arm over Mickey's shoulders the way a favorite uncle would while saying goodnight to a visitor. His fingers tightened on Mickey's upper arm to hold him in place, and Mickey broke out in a sweat, suddenly afraid that --

The thought never finished forming in his mind. The instant Blaine turned his back to stride into the woods Flag threw his hunting knife with deadly aim.

Mickey's horrified scream was stifled by Flag's other hand covering his mouth, and then Gary was grabbing his wrists from behind to tie them.

Sport raced to stand in front of the fallen ranger's body. His teeth were bared in a menacing snarl and Flag grabbed his revolver to snap, "Control that mean animal or he's as dead as Kern!"

Gary was wrapping a line around Mickey's ankles and he fell to his knees as he gasped, "Sport, stay!"

The dying ranger gave a heartrending moan and Gary said dully, "Close your eyes so you won't see the blood."

But Mickey's eyes were frozen open, and the grisly sight of Flag making sure that Blaine Kern would never tell anyone anything was carved into his brain for all time.

A totally cowed Sport slowly crawled on his stomach to press his trembling body close to Mickey's and Gary wept as he insisted, "They're only wrestling, Sport. Don't worry, Flag will win."

Mickey's supper erupted in a flood. He couldn't stop retching after his stomach was empty and Gary sighed to say, "I guess you're as blood-chicken as I am."

Flag rose from the murderous deed to growl, "Kern outsmarted himself, Mickey Mouse. Pretending it was a church picnic while the two of you sent secrets with your eyes! I'm gonna stuff that dishrag down that rotten dog's throat! Blaine Kern never asked one question I expected, not even about that neon sign around your skinny middle! Hell, you're wearing a jacket with his name sewed in it!

People who don't ask me the questions I'm ready for get my answer anyway!"

Striding to jerk Mickey's belt from around his waist, he snarled at Gary, "One bead at a time; I don't care what you spell with it! And the only trick 'Smort' is going to do from now on is Dead Dog!"

Mickey sobbed, "God damn you, Flag! I pray you burn in hell!"

Flag suppressed his fury and answered with icy calm, "Your trouble is you pray when you should be getting organized. I don't know what made that nosy ranger come up here, but if you're doing anything to leave a trail, you'll be digging pig graves from here to where I bury you."

"No trail," Mickey whispered, afraid that Gary would tell him about the sign on the rock facing the stream.

But Gary had either forgotten about their secret pact or he was afraid of breaking it. He only begged fearfully, "Flag, was the ranger alone?"

Flag smiled to comfort him. "I don't know, son, but now we've got three hostages, and if there's a posse out there, they don't know that one of them is dead. If the pigs demand proof, we'll send Sport out first, wearing Mickey's belt around his bloody neck."

Chapter Nine

"Come on, take the pills."

Mickey's head turned away from Gary's soft, insistent order and Gary coaxed, "It'll make you feel better. I always take two tranquilizers after I see blood. Besides, Flag said you have to. Please, Mickey, I don't want him to have to come in here and cram 'em down your throat."

"Where is he?" Mickey whispered through dry, cracked lips. He craved the water Gary held out to him, but the strong drug made him feel like he was already dead.

Gary sighed. "Burying the garbage. Listen, Mickey, nobody's out there or all hell would've busted loose."

He sounded like he was reassuring a friend instead of killing his last hope and Mickey pleaded, "Just give me the water and I'll play possum. Please, Gary, the pills will only make me sicker."

"No they won't!" Gary said stubbornly. "They'll make you relax and forget everything. I'm taking care of you, like Flag said. Now open your mouth!"

"He's going to k-kill me." Mickey began to shake with fear that he would never wake up. "Where's Sport?"

"Watching for cops!" Gary lost patience with him. "Flag promised not to kill you unless you betray us again."

Flag asked from outside the tent, "Won't he mind you, Gary? Do you need me to do it?"

Gary whispered, "Hurry up and take the pills!" He pulled Mickey's head back by his hair as he answered, "He's taking them, Flag."

Mickey let Gary put the drug in his mouth and wash it down. Some of the water spilled on his jacket, *Blaine's jacket*, and helpless tears of grief rolled down his cheeks.

Gary's eyes watered and he begged, "God, don't cry! Flag won't put up with that for a minute. He says if I can't keep you under control he'll be forced to put you out of your misery. Don't even whine, Mickey, or he'll say I should have kept the dog for a pet instead of you."

"A pet?" Mickey's teeth chattered and he started to shake with chills. "Gary, I'm a human being."

"I know that. You're my blood brother." Gary nodded in solemn agreement. "But wasn't Sport your best friend, even if he was a pet? I'll treat you as good as you ever treated your dog, and Flag promised to get us a new puppy who'll know I'm his master when we get to Hong Kong."

"You're not keeping Sport." Mickey already knew the answer. Sportin' Life would be buried with Blaine Kern.

"We didn't bring enough food for four!" Gary quoted Flag like a mindless robot. "I don't like it any better than you do, but we're dead-meat if we don't stick to our plan."

Mickey argued desperately, "Sport can hunt his own food. He can find game if we run out of food. He can kill rabbits, and even snakes."

"I know that!" Gary wept telling him, "But Flag says you and Sport are like an arrow pointing to each other and we can't change the color of a dog's hair. So just be glad he's letting me give you my table scraps."

Mickey gave up. Maybe Gary was insane, not just re-tarded. The Chasen brothers had never learned right from wrong and the depression that hit him as the drug dulled his senses made him almost wish he wouldn't wake up.

***

His drugged mind crawled through the cave or fooled around in Overland Park with his friend, Hodge. Loyal Sport ran through his dreams and Mickey relived the experience of drowning.

Arousing from his stupor to find that he was still alive, he realized he had been more willing to give up in Simpson's Hole than he was now. Life had become more than dear, and taking Gary's downers were intensifying his anger and hatred. He had gained a purpose.

He was living for one reason above all; to see Flag Chasen lose and get what was coming to him. He wet his lips to mumble, "What did you do with my dog?"

Flag answered from a hazy distance. "I gave him an even chance, which is more than I'd do for most humans. I left him tied to a tree."

Mickey's teeth gritted and the pounding in his head increased as he said, "He'll get loose."

Flag had made his first mistake. Sport could chew his way through a stupid rope in less than an hour. He would go for help and then track them down step by step.

"Sport's smart," Gary agreed optimistically. "Even snow chains won't keep him there."

Mickey's hope died. Flag had chained Sport where the bobcats would kill him. The stupefying drug took over and the lines binding his ankles and wrists became chains.

***

Time passed as it had in the cave, with day dissolving into night. Whenever Mickey woke up enough to know what was happening Gary would give him something to eat and make him take another tranquilizer.

69

Flag cut his hair and bleached it a sickly blond shade. Gary toweled it dry as if he was a dog and Flag joked, "Don't feed your mouse too well or he'll get strong enough to run away. Let Mickey adjust to his new situation and we'll see how he does."

Mickey mumbled, "When you put me out of my misery will you give me an even chance?"

Flag smiled to answer, "I'll see that you don't suffer. Are you suffering?"

"Not enough," Mickey growled. "Maybe I'll adjust."

He licked scraps of meat off a plate with his curling tongue and wondered how long Gary would stay mad at his brother for killing the only friend he ever had.

After he was brought back in the tent after going to the bathroom he decided to tell Flag, "Gary's taking good care of me, even if I never get to go for walks or do tricks."

Gary giggled at the thought of Mickey doing tricks and then he worried, "Mickey's not getting enough exercise."

"Smart mouth." Flag's eyes narrowed at the hostage he had kept for insurance against lawmen and he taunted, "Finish your meat, Mouse, and try not to think about how some helpless animal died to feed you. What makes you think that a man has a soul and a rabbit doesn't? Or a cow, or a fish. Don't you think they had friends who miss them while you sit there eating them?"

The meat stuck in Mickey's throat as Flag said scathingly, "If a man doesn't die, but goes to heaven or is reborn, how do you know he won't come back as a lamb? How do you know that you're not eating your great grandfather? What's so different about killing a ranger who's plotting your death from killing a pack of wolves who'd tear you limb from limb? In my book that's *self-defense*, Mister Barnes. I never killed anyone who didn't want me dead; and if I have to kill you, that'll be the reason."

Gary nodded sadly, unable to argue with Flag's logic, and popped a tranquilizer.

Mickey was afraid to want Flag dead. He tried to tell himself that the pain Flag would inflict wouldn't last any longer than the panic he had felt when he was drowning and then he would drift off to sleep. But his memory of dying didn't comfort him, because Flag would go on living and killing. He would keep poisoning the dumb animal who was his brother.

In Mickey's book, Flag had to suffer. He had to admit that he had made mistakes and take the consequences. Death was too good for Flag. Hell would welcome him with open arms. *What could make Flag Chasen suffer the way he had made others suffer?*

Mickey vowed to hang onto life long enough to leave a scar that would never heal. He would make Gary's memories of the months they had spent together in the Rocky Mountains so unforgettable that Flag would end up hating himself for not keeping his promise to let Mickey Barnes be their brother.

***

The tent was loaded and everything was piled into the jeep. Gary had eased off on the tranquilizers because Mickey had started to smile stupidly and fail to respond except to scratch himself and yawn. He had been exercised briefly before being dumped into the jeep and his limpid brown eyes had thanked his master like a devoted dog.

Gary was concerned about his best friend's inhuman behavior and Flag said, "Don't worry. He's probably just going through a stage."

Mickey mumbled in Gary's ear twenty minutes later, "Have t'go." If Flag wouldn't stop the jeep, he would let go all over the duffel bags like a puppy that was too doped-up to have any control. Gary would cry when Flag whipped

71

him, especially if he didn't shed a tear. Flag would be hurting inside, even if he didn't show it.

Gary lied, "I guess I drank too much coffee with breakfast. I need to stop again."

Flag ordered, "Empty your mouse's bladder while you're at it, but don't be too long."

The weather was getting cooler. Summer had turned to autumn and the forest was so beautiful that it hurt to see. Deep green foliage accented the red leaves on the trees, and scampering woodland creatures were preparing for the coming of winter. A fat squirrel ran up a tree with a nut in his mouth and Gary said, "Look, Mickey, isn't he cute? Flag, do we have any nuts to give him?"

Flag's reply was predictable. "You don't give nuts to squirrels, son, you take nuts from squirrels."

He grinned at his wisdom and Mickey nodded to say, "That makes sense." The squirrel was doomed.

Flag's eyebrow rose suspiciously and he pointed out, "You take honey from bees and pick berries off of trees."

"And make milk into cheese," Mickey smiled stupidly. "And dogs give us fleas."

It didn't surprise him when Flag laughed and made a few more rhymes to make him look superior at the game. Flag was unaware of the serious game Mickey was playing. It hadn't occurred to him that Gary could forget simple rules like setting the brake on the jeep, but he would remember how much fun it had been to camp out in the mountains with Mickey for the rest of his unnatural life.

That night as they sat by glowing embers to shell stolen nuts Mickey offered, "I could make a neat hat out of that squirrel fur that'll last forever."

"You can? That's great!" Gary ran to bring it to him.

Mickey apologized, "The trouble is I'd need a knife, and Flag's probably afraid I'd try to hurt him with it."

Flag laughed lazily. "Listen, Barney, when I start being afraid of a mouse I'll take up a new occupation." He tossed over the pocketknife that had been in Blaine's jacket pocket and ordered, "Make Gary's hat and we'll pin the squirrel's tail on your pants so you can wag it."

Mickey swallowed bitter hatred and winked at Gary to say, "A tail is for wagging; a bark is for bragging." Then he decided to add, "A wife is for nagging," because Flag's bite was a hundred times worse than his bark.

***

In the early morning hours just before dawn, the sound of repeated barking disturbed Mickey's sleep. He opened his eyes thinking it was another dream. This wasn't the first time he had imagined the sound since the Golden Retriever had been left chained to a tree. Sport had barked that way after he swam out of the Green Mist Pool, commanding Mickey to jump.

The distant barking continued and Mickey sat up to listen intently. That didn't sound like a coyote or a wolf. It was Sport! He had gotten away and he was following them from a safe distance, challenging Flag to come and get him. He was giving a murderer an even chance.

"Mickey?" Gary whispered. "Do you hear barking?"

"I always hear barking, Gary." Mickey said sadly, "When you love someone, you keep hearing them forever and ever after they die."

"On the level, Mickey?" Gary worried.

"I swear to God." Mickey vowed to make Gary keep hearing his words longer and louder than his brother's.

Flag lit a candle and his head tipped in the way Mickey had learned to dread. Then he gave a nod and said, "Sounds like we've got company, boys." He didn't sound afraid even though Sport might have brought an army with him.

His eyes were dancing in the candlelight as he said, "Let's get organized, son."

"Now?" Gary was sleepy. "Couldn't we wait until--"

"He who hesitates burns, remember?" Flag was more excited about going into battle than annoyed by having his sleep disturbed.

The full artillery came out and Mickey's hands and feet were tied by an apologetic master who promised him, "It's only until we know it's safe to go back to sleep."

Gary sighed and told Flag, "I'm sorry I didn't let you kill the dog. You were right about not taking chances." More afraid of being arrested than Mickey was of dying, he made sure that his pills were in his pocket to insure that he wouldn't be taken alive.

"Gotta be a different dog," Flag muttered. "Cops wouldn't let a dog announce their arrival that way -- unless they want me to come into the woods after him and leave his little buddy unguarded. Uh-uh, no... I'm not buying."

The barking came closer and Mickey laughed telling Gary, "Maybe Sport's going to stay just out of reach and keep barking his head off to drive us crazy. When you get a new puppy you'll need to have his bark removed."

Flag snapped, "Shut up and listen!"

Mickey put his finger to his lips and looked at it cross-eyed. Gary giggled, and Mickey bet that Flag was starting to regret not killing him on the night they met. It wouldn't be long before he learned that his sedated hostage wasn't as dim-witted as he thought.

Chapter Ten

"Come a little closer, boy," Flag whispered and held his rifle ready with the silencer in place.

They had seen Sport's lean body race through the trees not more than a hundred feet away in the early morning mist and Flag's first shot had misjudged the dog's speed.

Mickey was tied to a tree near the tent and he thrilled to the sight of the Golden Retriever whose cleverness scorned chains and knew how to get a murderer's goat.

He bragged recklessly, "You can't kill him, Flag, that's only Sport's ghost. He was devoured by wild animals."

No one could kill Sportin' Life. He was immortal, and it would take more than Flag high-powered rifle or Gary's drugs to destroy the force that kept Sport and Mickey alive.

"A ghost!" Gary breathed as they glimpsed the dog too briefly for Flag to take aim. "That's what he looks like."

"Gary, shut up!" Flag snarled, irritated beyond endurance. "Will you let me think?"

His plan hadn't allowed for an immortal Golden Retriever that was hell-bent on driving him insane and he muttered, "That rotten beast is as alive as I am, but I'll never for the life of me understand why."

Mickey dared to say, "He loves me. We're friends, and he'll always find me. You can kill a person's best friend, but you can never kill their memory."

Now Sport seemed to be barking from behind them. His bright-throated challenge was echoing off a high rocky ledge and the sound had a metallic, mocking ring. It was impossible to tell where he was and Mickey closed his eyes to listen to the wonderful sound.

Flag ordered Gary, "Untie Mickey."

"What for?" Gary asked, "What are you going to do?"

Flag growled, "I'm going to bait a hook and make Mister Barnes eat that miserable pup!"

Gary paled, believing every word, and he pleaded, "Oh, Flag, please don't!"

"Untie him," Flag commanded. "Mind me, Gary."

Mickey told Gary as he hesitated, "Your brother's jealous of me. He's never going to get you a puppy because it would remind --" His head snapped back as he was kicked in the face. Pain tasted like warm blood and Mickey gritted his teeth to say, "Remember me."

Gary chattered, "I'm untying him! Don't whip him!" His swimming eyes apologized to Mickey for not being able to save his life.

Flag shouted, "I've got Mickey Barnes, and I'm taking him with me alive if you get the hell out of here! If I don't get an answer in one minute I'm going to carve my initials in his back!" He put down the rifle to pick up his knife. Holding the revolver in his left hand, he ordered Mickey, "Stand up and take off your shirt."

The pain was going to last longer than Mickey had bargained for and he was afraid that Sport would attack. The dog had stopped barking, probably because he was coming closer, and Mickey reminded Flag as he unbuttoned his shirt with icy fingers, "You promised Gary that I wouldn't suffer. He'll never forget what you did to me."

Gary covered his face with his hands to sob, "I don't like you, Flag! Cut me if you have to hurt somebody. I'm the one who made you give Sport an even chance."

Flag rasped, "Can't you see that he's trying to make you hate me? Mickey wants us to fight. He wants to kill me." The point of the knife touched Mickey's bare chest as he yelled, "Twenty seconds!"

"Since when could I kill you?" Mickey pushed bitter words through numb lips. "Gary knows you're a liar, Flag."

The knife pierced his skin and Gary shrieked, "Don't kill him! I can't stand any more blood!" He dropped down to hug Mickey around the knees. "Please, Flag, no!"

Through a white haze that was threatening to make Mickey lose consciousness he could see that Flag was afraid to kill him. He wet his stiff lips to tell Gary, "Don't look, it'll make you sick. Take a tranquilizer and dream of all the fun we had."

A glint of admiration crept into Flag's ice-blue eyes and he murmured, "You never give up, do you, Barney? But I'd be a fool to --"

Sport's attack was silent and perfectly timed. Before they knew he was there he sprang into the air to knock Flag backwards. Sinking his teeth into Flag's wrist to make him drop the knife to the ground, Sport yelped with pain as the revolver whipped up to fire. He fell to his side with blood oozing from his head and his eyes glazed over, then closed and he lay still.

Mickey roared with fury and charged, determined to fight for his life as long as there was breath left in his body. He kicked the knife away and Flag wrestled him easily to the ground. The snub-nosed revolver was aimed at Mickey's throat and he tried to push it away as Gary screamed, "No, Flag, no! I'll hate you for killing him!"

Flag only hesitated for an instant before the gun was discharged in a deafening explosion. Gary howled like an abandoned wolf cub and Mickey waited to feel the searing pain. He didn't know where he had been hit, and then Flag fell backwards with blood gushing from his chest.

Terrified that the battle wasn't over, Mickey picked up the gun to take aim and pull the trigger. Flag's body gave a spasmodic jerk and his anguished expression went blank.

In the terrible silence that followed, Mickey couldn't help saying, "Poor bastard."

"Flag?" Gary's hands came slowly away from his face and he repeated, *"Flag?"*

He stumbled forward to drop to his knees and stare into his brother's unseeing eyes. Astonished, he asked, "Dead?" as if Mickey must be God or the devil.

Flag looked like an ordinary man in death, not half as tough as Blaine Kern, and Mickey said, "He lost."

"No, no!" Gary panted hysterically, choking on his words. "You cheated, Mickey! Flag was right, you wanted him dead!" His eyes rolled and he looked like he would faint. Then he grabbed up the knife to yell, "You were making me mad at my brother so you could kill him! And I let you do that!"

Mickey backed away to say, "Gary, we'll be okay --"

"You're not my blood brother anymore, Mickey Barnes!" The knife waved wildly in Gary's hand. "You're not my friend, you're nothing but a stupid pig cop!"

He ran at Mickey with the knife held high and screamed, "You want me locked up in the crazy house!"

The gun was still in Mickey's hand. His finger was on the trigger and shooting was instinctive, as if he had planned this moment in his drugged dreams.

Gary's body whirled away with his arms flung high, and then he crumbled to the forest floor with his hands reaching toward Flag. His eyes closed and his face became peaceful in death.

Mickey moaned and threw the gun away from him. His knees buckled and his brain threatened to explode with guilt as he wept, "God, oh God..."

It was true that he had wanted Flag dead, but never Gary. Turning his face away, he knew he would never stop seeing their still bodies lying in the dirt in front of the tent. He would wonder until he died why the Chasen brothers had appeared in the forest to kidnap a lost teenager before he could make his way to a ranger station.

He looked at the motionless Golden Retriever and his mouth twisted in grief at the loss of the truest friend he had ever known.

Sport uttered a noise that sounded like a yawn and his tail flopped on the ground. His eyes blinked uncertainly, as if he were asking why he wasn't dead, and Mickey whispered in awe, "Are you a ghost?"

Appearing just long enough to destroy Flag's plan, would Sport run off to vanish among the trees?

No, ghosts didn't bleed from a bullet wound in the head. Crawling to the dazed dog on his hands and knees, Mickey saw Flag's hastily aimed bullet embedded in a tree trunk behind him. The center of the Golden Retriever's head had been seared by the hot lead as if Flag had carved his initials, but Sport's amazing brain had escaped injury.

Mickey's head lowered to rest on Sport's warm body and he wept with gratitude, "We're both immortal, and no one's ever going to treat you like a dumb pet again."

As soon as Mickey was able to stand up and walk he went to get the medical kit from the jeep. He was wearing a wool sweater and Blaine's jacket over his shirt, but he was still shivering with cold as he chattered, "We'll keep the wound clean and coat the rawness against the open air so it will heal. There's something in this kit for infection, if I can just remember -- Oh, here it is."

He didn't want to think about infection and he told the patient Retriever, "You'll probably have a scar, but maybe it'll give you a distinguished look. For sure you'll look tough. Nobody's going to argue with a dog who can live through something like this... Hey, you're tough, Sport, and they don't come any smarter. I almost had them believing that you were a ghost out there, do you know that?"

His laugh was a sob. "Hell, I believed it myself when you -- Listen to me swearing like a Chasen. I'd better watch that, Dad will never buy it. There now, you're taken care of.... I hope I'm doing the right thing. Not that my doctoring could kill you, but I wish --"

His eyes closed to hide his tears and words came hard. "I wish you could talk."

The awful stillness was making him want to scream and he panted helplessly for a minute before he could say, "Maybe I talk too much."

Sport's limpid brown eyes seemed to be saying whatever needed to be said and Mickey sighed. "Chuck says I never shut up. Dad says that's because I'm hyper, but I'll never get hooked on tranquilizers, no matter what. Drugs are nothing but a daily dose of suicide.... How not to be alive." He bit his tongue on the last word and it hurt terribly for a few seconds.

He sat with his head bowed, praying for numbness.

Time passed. The only sound in the forest was the wind in the trees and the chirping of birds. Then a frog croaked nearby and Sport whined as if he were trying to tell Mickey not to go to sleep.

He agreed huskily, "We can't sleep here... Need to move the tent. I'll be too tired later. If Gary could drive the jeep, I can. I'm as smart as--"

He realized with a sinking heart that that every trick he had used to sharpen Gary's memory of their time together was going to ricochet like a gunshot in a cave.

A moment later, making himself get the car keys out of Flag's pocket, he told the sympathetic Retriever, "We have to bury them, but all we've got is their sleeping bags."

He barely had the strength to pick up the shovel and he said grimly, "That can't be any harder than making ourselves keep going in a cave. Here we've got blue sky and trees. I hope I never forget how it feels to be outdoors."

Putting their lifeless bodies in the sleeping bags gave him nausea and cramps, and Mickey muttered to Sport, "With any luck that's the last of the tranquilizers coming up. My stomach thinks we're having a nightmare, but this has to be real, because we'll never be able to do it again."

He put off digging the grave by finding a dozen things that had to be done first. That reminded him of the excuses he used to make to put off taking out the garbage and he whispered, "Garbage, oh no... God help me."

It was dusk by the time the Chasens were buried where they had fallen in the half-circle of rocks. Sport had trailed Mickey's steps until weakness and exhaustion made him flop down to rest by the shallow grave.

Each of the brothers had their most prized possessions with them. Gary's tranquilizers were by his hand and Flag's revolver, wiped clean of prints, was at his side. Mickey had wanted to give Gary his beaded belt, but that would have been like leaving a signed confession in the grave.

He found Flag's marking pen with the maps and printed *C H A S E N* on the face of a rock behind the double mound. Not sure what month it was, he added in smaller print *Brothers -- Autumn, 1979.*

The kindest thing anyone could have said about Flag and Gary was that they had been loyal brothers to the end.

Kneeling to offer a prayer, all he could think of was his gratitude that he and Sport were still alive. He finally said,

"God be with them. Protect Gary from Flag's temper and wash them clean if there's any way."

Rising, he confessed, "I hate leaving them like this, but they'll get more respect than they would in a cemetery."

The tall trees reaching up to the sky and the evidence of continuing life in the forest made it an eternal paradise that would change very little in the years to come.

He turned away from the graveside blinded by tears. Flag had been heartless, but if he had been raised by loving parents he might never have robbed or killed anyone. Since Flag had raised Gary, murder had seemed no more evil to him than killing a squirrel to make a fur hat.

Mickey told the sympathetic dog, "I was stupid to think I could take Gary to a doctor. He would have ended up in the crazy house like he said, and with his police record they never would have let him out. He's better off --"

That was what Gary had said about Angela. She was better off dead.

Mickey kicked angrily at something on the ground and saw that Flag's wallet had fallen from his pocket when his body was being rolled into the sleeping bag.

He muttered, "What do you know; I robbed a robber." *And killed a murderer.*

The name on the driver's license was Tom Morgan. Tom had no doubt given his life along with his license, and possibly his jeep.

There were fourteen fifty-dollar bills in the wallet. Gary's gambling dept was paid. Another bill was in the coin pocket, wrapped around something hard, and Mickey prayed as he unwrapped it, "A key?"

It was the kind of key Chuck had gotten at the roller rink when he rented a locker for their jackets and shoes. This key was for Locker 119, place unknown, wrapped in a fifty-dollar bill as if it might be important.

82

Mickey told Sport, "It's important, all right. This is where half a million dollars is stashed."

He stared at Flag's cash in his hand as he murmured, "Multiply this many, many times, and this little key will give it to you."

Chapter Eleven

"Does my jerky driving make you sick?" Mickey apologized to the dog lying lumped on the front seat beside him and Sport sighed in a wheezy admission that a head injury and jolting car motion were poor companions.

"Sorry about that." Mickey was retracing their route, using Flag's map whenever his memory was fogged because of Gary's drugs.

Afraid at first to drive, he had set his jaw and told himself that he was already so unstrung that nothing could make it worse. Driving the jeep kept him focused on moving in the right direction, and shifting gears gradually became easier going back over roads they had laboriously carved out. It was easier to remove the foliage that covered their trail than he had thought it would be. The few times he was unsure of the route, Sport's smart nose guided him.

It was a relief to be able to concentrate on something positive for a change. Dwelling on the facts of his escape could make him lose what was left of his mind. Whenever Gary's face floated over the dusty road to haunt him, he fought the illusion with the memory of being called Mickey Mouse and treated like a dog that needed to be tranquilized.

Finding that the jeep was registered to Tom Morgan made him glad that no one else would die by Flag's knife but it complicated returning to civilization in the jeep. Knowing that Flag and Gary had left him no choice didn't ease his guilt about how they had died, but his determination to remain in control of his fate was fortified by having won that battle.

As the sunlight began to fade Mickey was surprised to see that they were nearing the campsite where Blaine Kern was murdered, less than a month ago unless his mind lied about time.

He mused, "Building a road and covering it up must have taken us longer than getting anywhere."

A red line on Flag's map suggested an alternate route that would take them to a town faster, but there didn't appear to be a road. Mickey had a strong desire to drive to the ranger station at Miracle Falls and ask them to call his family, but he guessed it would be smarter to ditch the jeep as soon as he got close enough to walk. He was tempted to shove it off a cliff, but that might make him an accessory.

Turning on the headlights Flag had seldom used, he told Sport, "We'll stop pretty soon. Tomorrow we'll try to find out what they did with Blaine's body."

Pain twisted inside, remembering how the innocent ranger had died. Sport whined and Mickey said, "We owe him that much, and finding Blaine can't be any worse than a lot of other things we've had to do. Like Dad says, the rough deals in life are what toughen you up."

***

Scanning the campsite that had left a permanent imprint on his brain, Mickey was saddened not to find a plot of freshly turned earth that would indicate a decent grave.

He insisted, "Right here is where he died, I'm sure of it, but there's no blood on the ground. There isn't even a mark from our tent stakes. I must have slept through a lot of hard action."

85

Sport sensed that the search was over and he flopped down to rest. His nose had gone in ever-widening circles to look for the dead ranger but he had always ended up where the jeep had been parked.

Mickey sat beside him to agree, "Blaine's body was taken away in the jeep. We may never know where. It must be the worst thing in the world to lose someone you care about and never know where they ended up." That gave him another reason to make sure that they made it all the way home and he decided, "We need to leave a memorial of some kind so people will know how he died."

His eyes drifted over the terrain, visualizing a marker.

Blaine Kern was killed here by Flag Chasen Oct. 1979

The grisly scene flashed through his mind and he crossed his arms over his cramping stomach to say, "I must be hungry, I don't think I'm sick. Maybe I'm still unloading the miserable drugs and my body isn't sure what it wants. I need to drink a lot of water."

Giving himself parental advice, he asked Sport, "Do you want to help me fill the canteens or wait here?"

Sport stood up to go to the stream with him. They took it easy, doing things right, not fast, and the simple chore was so tiring that talking was an effort.

"Next time I'll let you fill your own canteen. I'll bet you could do that if I looped the strap around your neck. I'd have to fasten the lid, of course, but you can do a lot of things I can't, so that makes us equal."

They went back to the jeep and Mickey got out the marking pen. He felt he should offer a prayer when he finished the memorial for Blaine, but it seemed more important not to be found here. He needed to be in control of the time and place when it became known that Michael Barnes was not among the missing.

***

86

Sleeping curled close to Sport, he dreamed about finding Blaine alive and well. In his dream Blaine shot it out with the Chasens, the way it should have been, and Mickey asked him, "Did you track me from where Gary and I wrote our names on the rock facing the stream?"

Blaine replied, "I came to caution some fool campers that they were in rough territory, then I saw too many clues to ignore. It was obvious that you were being held hostage, and who else but the Chasens would carve out a road instead of taking the highway?

"I had two reasons for messing up Flag's plans -- to get you home safely and to remove those rats from my forest. The Rocky Mountains have been my home and my church. This is where I do most of my living, and it's where I'll die, God willing. Mother Nature and I are best friends, like you and Sport. Whatever she does, I'll defend."

***

At noon the next day the jeep rounded a turn to join a dirt road that was just wide enough for a small vehicle. It felt smooth as glass compared to the rough trail they had been following and as they had a drink from their canteens Mickey celebrated by offering a toast.

"To Blaine Kern and his forest."

His dream had made him feel like the dead ranger was reaching out to comfort him from wherever he lay, and he told the attentive dog, "Mom and Dad think our bodies are out here too, but only because they can't see us. Maybe they have dreams, too."

An hour later the dirt road joined a two-lane highway. A huge boulder at the intersection looked like there ought to be a sign on it and Mickey wrote *BLAINE KERN FOREST* to declare the territory Blaine's permanent home.

He added an epitaph; *May Nature defend him for all Eternity* and told Sport, "That will lead searchers to the place where he died and let them know how it happened."

Sport started to lift his leg at the base of the landmark and then he went to a nearby tree instead. Mickey's laughter sounded almost natural in spite of the huskiness that reminded him of his father's voice after a hard day at work.

Walking back to the jeep, he sat quietly for several minutes before he decided, "I don't think I'll ever tell anyone anything about this trip. If Blaine and the Chasens are found and then the rock where Gary and I put our names, everyone will know I was in on the whole thing. But until that insane puzzle gets put together, we'd be smarter to act like we got hit in the head and can't remember a thing."

He frowned at the scab forming on Sport's head and realized that the hair might never grow back where Flag's bullet had seared a crease. He sighed to admit, "I don't know how to explain that. Or this..." His fingers pushed through his shaggy, straw-colored hair. "We're definitely a weird lookin' pair of critters to come drivin' down out of them thar hills."

Chapter Twelve

"Out of gas!" Mickey raged at his stupidity. "I thought those cans were full. Dammit anyway!"

That meant they were going to have to walk all the way to Miracle Falls, more than a hundred miles away! Neither of them was in any shape for that, and he knew he should have taken the alternate route even if it took a week to get to the north road. "We'd have found a gas station there, the way Flag planned. God, how can I be so dumb!"

Sport put his head between his paws as if he was being scolded and Mickey controlled his temper. "It's not surprising that I'm a blithering idiot after everything that's happened." His hand waved out of control insisting, "What the heck, we're lucky to be this far and have all this gear. We could probably pitch camp by the road and wait for someone to drive by."

That could be like waiting to be rescued in a cave.

Visualizing a skeleton lying by the useless jeep, he growled, "We'll walk down this road as if we were driving and before long we'll see someone." His tone hardened warning Sport, "We'll be careful about trusting anyone we meet -- especially strangers who offer me a cup of coffee."

Pitching the tent where he could keep an eye on the jeep, Mickey became aware of a strange gratitude toward his jailer as he determined what he would need. Flag had enjoyed lecturing 'the boys' about survival in the wilderness and a frightened hostage had memorized every word. Unfortunately, the most essential tools were the murderer's knife and the sharpener he had used daily.

The mechanical match was a necessary item, as well as the binoculars. The First Aid kit was vital, along with the maps and the light belt ax for chopping wood. The lightweight tarp would have to suffice in place of the heavy tent.

A down sleeping bag was a priority item, and the fishing kit that required cutting a pole as he went. Adding freeze-dried foods, a cooking pot and a few utensils to the collection Mickey told Sport, "You'll need a sleeping bag too if it gets freezing cold before we find someone."

They were partners, not a boy and his dog.

Looking around at his choices, Mickey wasn't sure if he would be able to lift the backpack if he could fit everything into it. A few emergency flares would have make all the rest unnecessary, but Flag had been better equipped to avoid rescue than to signal for it.

There were several items Mickey couldn't identify, but he guessed he wouldn't know how to use them anyway. Staring into a small zippered container, he realized that it was a snakebite kit. The extent of his ignorance was scary, and he would have traded his beaded belt for a copy of the Boy Scout Manual he had called a lot of BS.

He rationalized as he packed, "We could probably make it home even if we didn't have all this stuff. The worst thing that could happen would be for us to be mistaken for game by some hunter who's escaping to the woods to get away from his nagging wife."

Not sure if he was quoting Flag or his dad, he muttered, "Never mind. We'll eat now and turn in early so we can get a good night's rest. What are you scowling about?"

Sport barked at him and he apologized, "Sorry about that. I'm not used to seeing your scar and I can't tell if you're laughing or crying."

***

Bright morning and crisp cool air made restlessness return. Climbing a ridge to look down at the winding road, Mickey scanned the terrain beyond the jeep, trying to see something that would help him use the maps.

He said with disgust, "Nothing by trees and sky..."

Then he had to laugh. "There was a time, Sport, when trees and sky were more than enough. That goes to show that it depends on where you're standing to look. I'd rather die anywhere than a black, smelly cave, but we owe it to Blaine to get all the way home." He owed that to Flag too, but for a different reason.

Peering through the binoculars, he turned slowly as he promised, "If the airlines make you ride in a cage with the luggage, we'll walk to Kansas City. *Hey...*" He refocused the glasses and Sport stiffened, reflecting his hope.

"I see two roofs down there! Maybe three, with the sun shining on them. Cabin roofs, more than one. A settlement or a resort, I'm almost sure." His voice cracked saying, "Maybe it's a ranger station. Maybe that's where Blaine lived with--" *With his wife and children.*

His heart lost a couple of beats and then raced to catch up. What could he possibly say to Blaine's widow? How could he face her and pretend that he didn't know anything? He could only describe a cave in disgusting detail and pray that people wouldn't be surprised if everything that had happened since he got out was a blur.

If worse came to worst, he could always act crazy. The Chasens had been perfect teachers for that.

91

He stared through the binoculars telling Sport, "There doesn't seem to be much life around the place. Maybe it's a retirement home for old folks."

He had a terrible feeling that no one was there. It was either a closed summer resort or all the people were hiding from something, like a murderer on the loose.

"It's much too quiet," he murmured as he lifted off his backpack to conceal it in a bush. Relieved to be rid of the weight, he took a minute to stretch, and then something else struck him. The road seemed to have disappeared. It ought to lead to the settlement, but those cabins appeared to exist without any way to get to them.

"This is definitely strange... We'd better make sure we can find our way back to our supplies in case this turns out to be another dead-end. Do you understand? Find the pack, Sport, have you got that?"

Sport barked with excitement and Mickey cautioned, "Shh, save your voice for emergencies. Let's go quietly."

The closer they got to the silent settlement, the more unstrung Mickey became. What was worse than no houses at all was a bunch of vacant cabins, as if all the people had died of a plague or something.

What could have made the settlers go?

"A fire," he whispered as the charred remnants of the first cabin came into view. "A long time ago, because the trees here are either smaller or they're scarred. This was an old hunting lodge maybe, but it isn't now."

It looked like there might have been more than a dozen cabins at one time. A large common house was in the center, with only a foundation, two walls and a stone chimney. The people had left in a hurry, and Mickey steeled himself to find that some of them might not have gotten away. But only rotting, rusting evidence of a lost civilization was left. Neither he nor Sport found anything frightening or useful in the rubble.

Prowling from cabin to cabin, he remarked, "I'm surprised that Flag didn't think of holing up here -- unless this is the first place the police would suspect an outlaw of hiding out." His mouth was dry and his heart was beating too fast as he said, "It sure has a haunted look."

He turned over a wormy board with the toe of his boot. The word *'Office'* was carved on it and he said, "That's really old." Signs like that were mostly made of plastic now. "Two and a half cabins," he corrected his estimate, "and a dozen crumbling foundations."

He walked through what was left of the common house with its intact fireplace. "This place probably isn't even on the map anymore. There's no road -- look out, snake!"

They backed off to a safe distance when they heard the warning rattle. Grateful to Mother Nature for equipping rattlesnakes with built-in alarms, Mickey told the grouchy inhabitant that had slithered out of the fireplace, "We don't want your house, you can have the whole town. Nobody would want to live here but a snake."

The settlement was a dismal disappointment after their time-consuming detour and as they left he could only find one good thing to say about Snakesville. "At least nobody asked us any questions."

Sport gave a sharp bark, relieved to leave the ghost town behind and Mickey agreed, "Let's go get our gear. Where's the pack?" He started off in the wrong direction, pretending that he had forgotten where he had left it.

Sport retraced their steps to the pack on the hill and Mickey praised him, "Good going; good boy! Now do you know where the road is? Not the jeep, Sport, the way home; where Chuck is, and Mom and Dad." He kidded the listening Retriever, "But not as the crow flies, partner, because we still don't have wings."

Ten minutes later, consulting the map, he reasoned, "It doesn't matter which of these three cow-paths with the

93

dotted lines we take, because any of them will lead to a road, and sooner or later we'll come to a town."

After two hours he was forced to admit, "Either Flag's map is lying or it shows something that isn't there any more." There was one more possibility. "Or we've been walking in circles. That could be really upsetting if I let myself think about it. You know what? We're going to have to spend the night in the forest without a tent or a car."

Sport sat down and sighed. He seemed to be apologizing for not finding the way home and Mickey comforted him; "Staying with the car and the tent would have been just as dumb. We could have waited 'til snow fell, then froze to death clinging to our worthless tent and car. Firewood is all we need, and we know how to do that, right?"

There was no reason to panic; they weren't lost in a cave or held hostage by anyone. They were free, and the only enemy left to fight was winter.

Mickey insisted, "A hot supper and warm sleeping bags will change the way we feel. Tomorrow morning we'll head for Miracle Falls as fast as we can travel. We know that it's south, and the moss on the trees points that way if I remember right …

"Well, never mind, because we'll be able to see those gigantic falls from any mountaintop. There's all kinds of towns to the south, and it's not like either of us is crippled. We only ran out of gas, and we were planning to ditch the jeep anyway." Mickey took a deep breath before he added, "Flag was right when he said that whining about your bad luck only gets a guy left behind to rot."

Chapter Thirteen

"We've got two week's worth of food in the pack if we're careful. That ought to be more than enough."

Talking to the dog had become as necessary as sleep. The sun was their only compass and Mickey wished that he had learned how to navigate by using the stars at night. The trouble with a map was a person had to know where he was in order to use it.

When they stopped to rest he peered at it again. After a long moment he pointed to a discouraging nothingness that reflected their surroundings and mused, "I think we must be here. Because this is where we were when we ran out of gas and we've been traveling due south since we left Snakesville. That means we should be able to see Miracle Falls when we get to this ridge that looks like a dinosaur."

He decided to label the places he felt sure about, but with a pencil in case he had to change his mind. He named Kern Forest and wrote BK where Blaine had been killed. Labeling Flag and Gary's grave FGC, he put a JR where the jeep road had been carved out to join the dotted line on the map. After marking the paved road PR he put an X where he estimated that the jeep was parked. A wiggly line between Pinecrest and Miracle Falls indicated the cave system and he named their destination 'Dinosaur Ridge.'

He was hungry when he finished and it was too early for lunch. Making a difficult decision, he told Sport, "We need to save the dried foods, which you hate anyway, and catch as much game as we can. Preferably fish." *Squirrels were off-limits.* "If we could find a river we might be able to figure out where we are on this map."

The attentive Golden Retriever was listening to every word, and Mickey repeated, "Water, Sport, water. We need to find water, understand?"

Sport already knew that. Mickey was rationing their supply and he was thirsty. But that meant changing directions, so he headed east into the morning sun.

"Are you sure? Are you looking for water? Can you smell it?" If dogs could only shake their heads or nod to say yes or no, that would have helped so much!

Sport's nose lifted and he trotted off to find a drink.

It rained before they found a stream. Mickey caught the drops in his canteen as they trickled off a natural funnel on a rock face. Shivering with cold huddled in the hollow beneath the overhanging rock, he muttered, "I sure could use a little baby fat now."

Then he knew how Chuck would answer. "Well, get out the sleeping bags, dum-dum!"

Spreading the bags under the rock, he admitted, "I'm not crazy about the Granite Motel if you want to know the truth. Building fires in the rain is not my idea of fun."

Sport smelled like a wet wool rug lying beside him and Mickey couldn't help saying, "I hope wild animals hate rainy weather as much as we do. They'll be out in full force when it stops, and I bet nothing will burn then except pitch that turns our food black...

"Funny thing though," he yawned as he got warmer. "The thought of wild animals isn't as scary as it use to be. Wolves don't smile and act like they're starting to like you just before they attack. The animals around here act like they're more scared of us than we are of them, and you'll tell me if we've got company."

Sport barked several times during the night, issuing sharp, brittle warnings that showed he felt challenged. Whenever the alarm sounded Mickey made sure that the knife was handy. Wishing he could forget that it had killed Blaine, he knew that he should have brought the rifle. He had thought he would never be able to kill anything with it, and now he wished that they had returned to the jeep in order to follow the paved road to a town.

He rationalized that Flag's rifle probably had a criminal record and anyone who got caught with it would have a lot of explaining to do. Hunting without a license was against the law, and before long they would be back where law and order prevailed. That thought became a prayer and he slept with more confidence in tomorrow than he had known for months.

The bobcat that kept coming closer to increase Sport's nervousness never attacked. He sought a tree nearby, acting like his sanctuary had been invaded, and shrieked his indignation until morning.

After leaving his name on a marker to check out of the Granite Motel, Mickey discovered that the bobcat was too old to stand up for his rights. They caught a brief glimpse of their night caroler when he glared balefully at them before skulking off in the opposite direction as fast as his aging body could go.

Mickey said wryly, "I hope he doesn't send his grandchildren after us to get even. You and I could get pretty scratched up before we'd kill one of those mean babies. Even with two against one, their claws could do a lot of damage before the fight was over."

Sport gave a worried whine and Mickey told him, "Our most important job is to stay healthy and keep up our strength. From now on we're going to build a fire every night, even if we're tired enough to drop in our tracks. God, I nearly froze to death last night!"

The night air hadn't seemed that cold and he wondered if chills could be an emotional reaction. His mind kept replaying Blaine's murder and looking for ways that he could have kept that from happening. He would be willing to eat a snake if it would turn off his dreams at night.

***

The next morning he woke up feeling horrible. His throat burned and he ached in every joint. He moaned, "That's what comes of depending on tents and cars. I get a little wet and I catch a stupid cold!"

Taking in a breath, his chest stabbed with pain and he muttered with disgust, "If I push myself now I'll only get pneumonia. I hate to suggest this, Sport, but what we need is a nice dry cave. One we can walk out of in two minutes and don't have to evict someone with a stronger claim."

It was noon when they found a cave that contained evidence of a large, carnivorous inhabitant. Sport was anxious to leave, the smell of danger was putting him off, and Mickey murmured as they crept out, "Whoever lives here probably thinks it's a neat place. He'd take as kindly to our moving in as we'd feel if an bobcat moved in on us, and I'm in no shape to fight today."

He had been in worse shape on the morning Flag and Gary died. Between the lack of exercise, living on table scraps and being forced to take drugs, he couldn't have held his own against a bear cub. He might never know what had made Flag lose. Maybe that mystery was what was making him sick rather than the change in the weather.

They pushed on for shorter periods of time. The afternoon mist turned to a steady drizzle and Mickey could imagine Chuck razzing him that he could catch his death for being too dumb to come in out of the rain.

He mumbled, "Mom won't even let me fall asleep on the screen porch without covering me so I won't catch cold. I'm not that delicate. It's only a cold and a high temperature and I'm seeing things…"

That's how sick he was; he was hallucinating. He saw a beautiful little shelter ahead of them -- man-made, not created by any animal. Goosebumps rose on his arms and he rubbed at his eyes to say, "That's got to be an illusion."

It was a real lean-to, built from saplings that had been cut by a woodsman who knew what he was doing. A five-foot roof slanted to the ground to keep out the wind and rain, and the roof was covered with branches and bark that had been stripped from a nearby tree. There were remnants of a fire that had been laid to reflect the heat into the shelter, and a clever mattress of pine boughs had probably held a sleeping bag not long ago.

Mickey said reverently, "Either my guardian angel did this or it proves that we're not the only humans here! If someone comes back, we can talk to him instead of fighting over his shelter. He can't be any worse than a Chasen."

Blaine Kern might have built the sturdy little structure. It was obviously the work of someone who regarded nature as a friend. Unrolling his sleeping bag on fragrant pine boughs Mickey mused, "I bet I could build a place like this in less than an hour if I knew how to go about it. Sport, could you get some kindling? Firewood, okay?"

It was a humble request, not a command. He was too sick to order anyone around and Sport wasn't his slave. Hoping that the wood would be dry enough to flare up, he recalled Flag saying that birch bark never failed to burn.

As terrible as he felt, he was fascinated by how the spongy foliage kept his bedroll from touching the ground. He mumbled, "I could learn a lot by analyzing this shelter before we leave. It looks like he was pulling that log closer to the flame instead of bothering to chop it up."

Something else caught his eye and he stared at a stick that had been shaved to make thin ribbons of wood curl away like a fan. Reaching for it to get a closer look, he murmured, "I'll bet it was carved to make it burn faster."

Grateful for Blaine's pocketknife, he said, "We'll leave some of those fire-sticks behind and make a fresh mattress to thank whoever stays here, or for the next traveler who comes this way. The Angel Inn sure is a great improvement over the Granite Motel."

He realized that starting a guest list with his name and Sport's would help the ranger service find them, if anyone was still looking. He could add *'Headed for Miracle Falls.'*

The fire was burning by the time the drizzle turned to rain and Mickey told Sport, "If something edible runs by you could dash out and pick it up for breakfast. I won't complain if it's a squirrel. I'm afraid it's gotten to the point where it's him or us."

***

As the weather worsened Mickey's fever raged. It was all he could do to keep the fire going, and the sight of the snake Sport brought him for breakfast made him throw up.

He apologized for rejecting the Retriever's gift. "The way I feel now, I would have heaved at the sight of Mom's lasagna. All I need is a vitamin and some water."

The vitamins were nearly gone. It had become obvious that Flag was headed for a town where he could buy gas and replenish their supplies. Afraid he would never know how far away the town was Mickey moaned, "Is this the end of the road for me? I was never so sick in my life."

Maybe it only seemed that way. Lying in his bed at home with a family to care for him, common ailments hadn't been complicated by fear. Everything had been so easy at home. Mom would call, "Dinner's ready," and the house always smelled so good. There was gravy for the

100

meat, a big glob of mashed potatoes and a cold pitcher of milk. The family would sit around and watch television after supper while Chuck did his homework. Mickey's jokes had made them laugh more than the silly TV....

He prayed, "Lord, please don't let us die on this godforsaken mountain. What did I do to deserve this? Maybe it was something I didn't do."

He dreamed about coming home in the middle of the night. Sport refused to go in the house because he was an outdoor dog who was only allowed on the screen porch. They argued about where they would sleep and ended up building a shelter in the back yard.

Mickey's dad scolded him for not waking them up to announce that he was home and his mother wept with joy to see that they were still alive. Chuck came back from his paper route and Sport told him it wasn't fair that he had to sleep outside as if he were an ordinary dog.

Mickey woke to find that the sun was shining. His fever had broken and the Golden Retriever was watching over him the way his mother had when he was sick.

Sport stood up as if he were saying 'Lets go' and Mickey had to tell him, "I couldn't walk a mile. We'll have to stay here until I get stronger. If you haven't eaten your slimy snake yet, I'll skin it and cook it."

Sport went to push at the snake with his nose. Then he looked up at Mickey and his eyes were sparkling with fun.

"You're on, son." Mickey took the dare. "Chuck will never believe I ate a snake. Shall we take him the skin for a belt? He'd like that, it's really pretty."

Things like food and shelter certainly did depend upon a person's point of view.

Chapter Fourteen

A week of shelter building, fishing with Flag's illegal multiple line and eating stranger things than snake found the travelers camped on the ridge where Mickey had thought he would be able to see the falls. He could see a waterfall several miles to the east but it didn't look like Miracle Falls.

Bewildered, he muttered, "Maybe that's Metedeconk Falls, which is higher but has less water in it, I think."

Sport flopped down to rest and Mickey gave a shrug to add, "Oh well, there's probably a town there and I'm not going to be stubborn, except about one thing."

He knew if he couldn't make a plan and stick to it they might be trapped by winter. The weather had gotten colder than he could believe, and the thought of spending a snowy winter in the mountains was unimaginable.

He said, "Since there's no road we'll have to follow Dinosaur Ridge so we can keep the falls in sight. It's maybe sixty miles, two or three days of hard walking unless we hit a snag." He refused to think about snags. "If we have to look for water, we'll come back to the ridge afterwards. If rain provides water we might be less comfortable, but we'll be healthier when we get to the ranger station."

He knew that hunger would drive them on unless they ran out of energy, and he prayed that it wouldn't snow. The hunting had been bad and he couldn't sit and fish for hours when they could be getting closer to home. The fires they had built every night could have been seen for miles if any conscientious ranger had worried about fool campers risking their lives in dangerous territory.

Mickey cursed himself for having been an inferior Boy Scout who hadn't learned to signal for help. A small plane had flown overhead and after waving frantically he had tried flashing a mirror. The pilot had only dipped his wings in a friendly hello before disappearing in the distance.

Reality was changing its meaning. Weariness, fear and hunger were making a resentful mountaineer camped on a blustery ridge lonelier than he had ever imagined anyone could be. A chronic state of anxiety had replaced Mickey's gratitude for his freedom, and his impatience with the unending journey made him short-tempered.

Sportin' Life echoed his frustration. Several meals had gotten away from him and the campsite Mickey had chosen was less protected than he preferred. Gathering wood for a fire had always meant cooking supper, but now there was nothing to cook. They had been without food all day except for a few wild berries, and Sport had turned up his nose at those wet red things.

He expressed his feelings by refusing to gather kindling and Mickey had to remind him, "Fetch some wood."

The dog sat down and pouted.

Mickey ordered, "Go get some wood. We need a fire."

Sport flopped down and turned his head away.

"Don't pull that routine on me. I'm tired, too. All right, dammit, I'll help!" Mickey got out the light ax and began to chop firewood. "You have to carry it," he said peevishly.

Sport's head lifted. He stood up to raise his nose and sniff at the air. Then he bounded off into the trees to chase down the smell.

Mickey tensed with hope, then he muttered suspiciously, "If he's only trying to get out of helping with the chores, I'll smack him one."

Sport was gone for more than an hour. Mickey's hope increased and then turned to worry. The fire burned, the shelter had been built and their beds were made before the dog finally returned. He was carrying a small bird in his mouth, hardly enough food for one, and Mickey said with disgust, "Wow, don't tell me that's what you smelled and went tearing off to kill. Bring it here."

Sport dropped his kill where he stood and nosed at it.

Mickey commanded, "Give it up." The bird was hardly worth plucking and when he went to reach for it Sport grabbed the bird to pull it away.

"Oh, really. It's all yours?" Mickey asked, "Because you're too squeamish to eat berries? Come on, we're in this together, remember? Give me that rotten bird, dumb-bell! Do you want to eat the feathers?"

Sport backed away with the bird and Mickey scolded, "Did you bring it back to eat in front of me? I'm hungry too, dammit. Let go!"

Feathers flew as they fought over the foolish catch, and then Sport picked up the bird and ran into the forest with it.

Mickey tore after him. Hunger had sharpened his anger and Sport's selfishness hurt him beyond belief. Unable to see in the dark, he ran into a low-hanging branch and yelped with pain as he tripped over an exposed root. Falling forward, his head struck the tree trunk and he knocked himself out cold.

Everything floated away. Anger, hunger, and determination to win melted in a reddish-brown mist.

104

He came to lying on his back on the cold ground. A monstrous weight lay on his chest, anchoring his body to the floor of the forest as if he were buried beneath the soil. Betrayed by the only friend he had in the wilderness, he could barely breathe to whisper, "Sport, what are you doing to me? Get off, will you?"

The big dog sprawled on top of him let out a long wheezing moan.

"Get off," Mickey sighed. "I'm not dead. Come on; eat your stupid little bird. I don't want it." He had taken for granted that they would share the measly meal and he was ashamed to admit, "I wasn't treating you right."

He had ordered Sport around like a slave and called him names, which he had sworn never to do. He had behaved like an insensitive Chasen, assuming that it was a dog's duty to catch the food and a human's right to cook and eat it. He deserved to be smacked in the head.

He sat up dizzily to ask, "Would you rather eat it raw?" It didn't seem fair to have to cook the catch and not get to share it.

Sport crept a few feet away to lie facing Mickey with his nose between his paws.

"Hey, forget it." Mickey rubbed at his throbbing head. "It's not worth fighting over. Nothing is."

Crawling to the inconsolable Golden Retriever on his hands and knees, he remembered feeling that weak when he thought that Sport had been killed along with Flag and Gary. His hand drifted over the friend who had been lying on an unconscious companion for god-knows how long, afraid that he would never wake up.

Mickey said, "I'm not that hurt. Don't punish yourself." Hoping he hadn't gotten a concussion he said, "I was asking for a hit, and a guy might as well run at top speed in a cave as tear around in the forest on a moonless night."

Sport whimpered unhappily and Mickey begged, "Just eat your supper, will you?"

His swimming eyes located the bird with difficulty and he thought *stupid little beady-eyed bird. Five skinny bites; not even worth laughing over.*

He coaxed the dog, "Why don't you go get it, okay?"

Sport brought the bedraggled foul to Mickey to drop it in his lap. Then he flattened himself on the ground, looking away from the meal he refused to share.

"Oh for crying out loud." Mickey brushed away his tears. "'You didn't hurt me. I ran into a tree."

Sport began to pant softly and Mickey asked, "Are you crying?" Kneeling beside Sport to peer into his eyes, he was amazed to see a tear roll down the dog's long nose.

"Oh, Sport," he wept with him. "I forgive you."

He put his arms around the Retriever to tell him, "What's important is we're still alive and we're together, not one skinny little bird. I've been mean today; we've both been rotten. We'd rather be home and it seems like we're getting further away. This might not be the only fight we'll have. We can't read each other's minds. You can't talk, and I talk too much. I love you; that's all. Can you feel that?"

Sport's head lifted and he peered into Mickey's eyes as if he were repeating his words in a stronger, simpler way.

I didn't mean to hurt you. I got scared when you didn't wake up. Love is more important than winning.

Mickey nodded and answered silently; *I've been talking when I should have been listening.* He knew that Sport heard him, but he couldn't have begun to explain how.

It turned out that there were eight bites on the plucked bird, four apiece.

***

A beaver had gotten trapped beneath a small tree when it misjudged the direction of its fall. The meal that morning was the best they had eaten for a week, and after Mickey's hunger had been satisfied he could say philosophically, "One thing about cold weather, meat doesn't spoil as fast. It won't be long before we'll have the world's biggest freezer. Then I'll have to wear a beaver hat with ear muffs and learn to build an igloo."

Sport's head tipped as if questioning the strange word.

"A house made of snow and ice." Mickey's hands described the shape of an igloo. "Blocks, like cement, but with packed snow, and maybe water to seal it.... What I don't know is where the fire should be and how much fresh air we'd need."

He didn't chatter nervously the way he had at the start of their journey. Knowing that he wasn't just talking to himself made him choose his words with more care. His huskiness seemed to have become a permanent condition, but that could be due to tension or a deepening voice.

"If the walls were solid ice we'd have to make sure we were getting enough oxygen." Just thinking about it made Mickey shiver, and he mused, "How do the Eskimos keep the roof from falling in? Maybe the snow in Alaska makes better blocks than it does in the Rocky Mountains."

He realized that they could freeze to death before he learned to make an igloo and he said, "I need to think about what we'll do for shelter if we don't find a town before we get caught in a snowstorm."

A dry cave would be best, but that could mean living in it for months, with fishing streams iced over and game impossible to find. He would need snowshoes to walk through the heavy drifts, and the whiteness might be as blinding as being lost in a cave.

Sport's whine echoed his anxiety and Mickey said grimly, "I used to poke fun at the Boy Scout motto. Now 'Be Prepared' sounds like the best advice in the world."

Sport put his paw on Mickey's knee and his brown eyes were asking 'Are we all right?'

Mickey had to admit, "I don't know. I should have brought the rifle." He could have shot a hibernating bear.

That would be almost as evil as knifing a man in the back, but only something like a bear could provide them with enough meat for the winter.

**

Whenever Sport ate greens Mickey sampled them. He found weedy foods that eased hunger and balanced the rich meat of the beaver. When in doubt about strange fruit he would take a tiny bite and wait to see if it made him sick before eating any more. Tree bark and twigs became toothbrushes or chewing gum; nuts were exciting delicacies, and the only food he refused to take a chance on was mushrooms. According to Flag, a trial taste of a toadstool could mean instant death.

The moment Mickey had dreaded descended when they weren't more than two day's journey from a town he believed to be Metedeconk Falls. Sport's nose got him in trouble on the same night they were trapped by a snowstorm on Dinosaur Ridge. Thinking that he had found another easy meal like the beaver, he triggered a hunter's trap

Working desperately to free him from the steel claws, Mickey could see that Sport's paw was so badly mangled that he wouldn't be able to run and hunt.

By the time the injury was disinfected and splinted the ground was covered with snow. They couldn't travel and they were without shelter.

Chapter Fifteen

Mickey growled, "Diabolical contraption!" He despised the trap and the unknown trapper! The sight of Sport's crushed paw struck a nerve in his heart and he felt like the red blood dripping onto the snow was his own.

Nauseated, he looked away, a nightmare flashing through his mind. Then he knew what Flag would have done if an invisible enemy had attacked them and he said, "We'll hole up in that circle of rocks. Shall I unload my pack and come back for you?"

Sport scrambled to his feet and started to lope on three legs, telling his partner to run with him.

As soon as they reached the rock enclosure Mickey got out the First Aid Kit. He panted for breath saying, "I'll bandage the paw as soon as we've got shelter. But first we have to make sure it won't get infected."

Sport seemed to be apologizing for his mistake and Mickey told him, "It's not like you were trained to avoid traps. You'll have to take it easy until your paw heals. Don't worry about food. I'll steal the jerk's trap or find a sleepy bear and club him on the head with my frozen backpack. Dad would probably tell us to make friends with the trapper, but anyone who'd choose to live in the wilderness in the dead of winter has got to be crazy or a criminal."

He cautioned Sport, "Don't try to help me. Just lie quiet and watch a master at work."

Cutting saplings to bend them across the rock enclosure to form a roof, he laced the structure with thick pine boughs and floored it with more of the same. He piled boughs higher along one side and spread out their sleeping bags, telling Sport, "To bed, son. Just lie there and keep me company while I install the stove. A small fire to begin with, until we find out what the space will support.

"Ah, air vent;" he remembered a basic rule. "We'll see which way the smoke wants to go through the roof."

He looked around to say, "The door has to be here, and since our bed is there, the stove has to be on the other side. If a snowdrift starts to pile up and seal us in, I'll tunnel around it and use it for a windbreak. See how smart I'm getting? Ah, our Home Sweet Home sign will go here."

Leaving his name wherever they camped had become a prayer to bring rescuers, but Mickey knew that their frozen bodies might lie beneath this final marker if no one came.

He told the worried dog, "At least drinking water is no problem. We won't have to boil it, and you can have all you want. Tonight I'll bait that mean trap with the last of our beaver meat, and tomorrow morning I'll run over and pick up something downwind. Isn't that wonderful? We have our own Downwind Supermarket. So smile."

Sport smiled weakly. Mickey gave his back a brisk rub and said, "Good boy; don't lose heart."

No, Sport had heart to spare. It was only his paw that was out of order.

Mickey said, "I'll bandage that as soon as I gather some wood and finish the house. With any luck, it'll keep out the cold."

Snow was already starting to pack on the woven framework and he knew that if the span was too wide and he hadn't balanced the support evenly the roof would cave in when the snow got heavy.

The finished shelter was seven feet deep and five feet wide. The tallest point was nearly six feet and sloped down to the smaller rocks of the natural enclosure. Mickey was perspiring from his sped-up efforts as he built a tiny fire on the lowest side and poked a hole in the roof for ventilation.

He told Sport, "I'll have to make sure we keep that open. I'm no woodsman, but I know that too much air is better than not having enough. If we have to choose between suffocating and freezing to death, let's go the natural way. Hey, you know what? It's getting hot in here."

He was amazed by how much heat the fire created. The cracks in the shelter were already sealing and he prayed, "Let it snow just enough to keep out the wind and wet."

Grateful for the heavy boots he was still growing into, he hung his jacket over the backpack to dry. Blaine's nametag caught his eye and he said ruefully, "I'm going to have to take that out. It could lead to questions when we get back to civilization." *Or even if they didn't.*

Reaching for the First Aid Kit, he said optimistically, "When the weather clears and the snow packs hard enough to travel, we'll get off the mountain."

Sport had three good legs and they needed to find a veterinarian who could make sure his paw healed properly.

Mickey catnapped with a long stick by his side to poke at the ventilation hole in the roof. He got up often during the night to make sure that their exit wasn't being sealed off, and by the time the sun rose on a white winter world, an amateur woodsman was feeling triumphant.

It was exciting to know that they could stay warm and dry while a snowstorm raged outside. The roof was holding well with nine inches of snow packed on it and Mickey began thinking of ways to strengthen it. It would be like be-

111

ing buried in an avalanche if the shelter caved in on them, and the only good thing anyone could say about that was that it might be a more peaceful way to go than drowning.

***

On his way to check the Downwind Supermarket Mickey was thinking that if a person were to make a list of all the hazards in the wilderness during wintertime he might lie down in the snow and go to sleep.

Sport's mangled paw would be at the top of the list. It was a serious problem that required planning and action, not fear, which was a worse enemy than snow. The shelter was the tightest he had ever built, and snow could be a blessing. It would provide water and insulation and keep meat fresh. Now all he had to do was kill something.

Snow quieted footsteps in the forest and minimized the smell of man. He was able to sneak up on a deer foraging for food, and the fact that a fawn was with the doe didn't make him hesitate for more than three seconds. The only weapon he had was the long knife, and he threw it in the moment the doe sensed his presence. She took off fast and Mickey saw that he had nailed the fawn. Necessity fought with sentiment and he killed the mortally wounded fawn with a second thrust of the knife.

As the fawn's eyes went blank in death he could hear Flag taunting, *Try not to think how some helpless animal died to feed you. Isn't that murder? In my book it's self-defense, Mister Barnes.'*

They were using the same book now, living the same animal existence, and Mickey tried to keep himself human by praying, "God forgive me and provide our needs."

He asked himself what the difference was between killing a fawn or encouraging Sport to kill a snake -- or buying a hamburger for that matter. Meat came from the

112

same source, whether a person looked it in the eyes or depended on someone else to do their dirty work for them.

He murmured as he looked for the fawn's mother, "I'm really sorry." She was gone, and his sorrow faded as his mouth salivated for the taste of sweet young venison, a delicacy he hadn't tasted since leaving the Chasens.

Butchering the skinned meat in preparation for freezing it was an even more satisfying exercise than building the snow shelter. Sport's appreciation of his catch wiped the last regret from Mickey's mind and he bragged as he prepared to dry the skin, "I'll bet I could make some moccasins if I had the right kind of needle and thread... or if I knew how to make a needle and thread. I sure was a dismal failure as a Boy Scout."

***

The snow continued to fall and Mickey made braces for the roof out of forked branches with the foliage trimmed off. Replenishing the bed and floor, he warned Sport, "If you hear the roof cracking, get out fast, understand? The backpack is by the door with most of our stuff in it and I'll grab the sleeping bags on my way out."

Giving the dog a gentle rub, he wondered if Sport was running a temperature. "Maybe it's too hot in here. Let's take a look at the paw. Is it getting infected?"

He didn't know what he would do if the paw had to be amputated. Sport gave an anxious whine and Mickey comforted him, "Hey, anyone who can get out of Flag's chains isn't going to be stopped by something like a smashed paw. People will be amazed to see us walk in alive and well after all this time. Maybe we'll even be famous."

He put a fresh bandage on the paw and cooked a piece of venison for supper. Sport ate a few bites and drank some water. Then they slept and Mickey had another dream about coming home.

The dream crackled into reality when he woke to hear the roof of the shelter groaning beneath the weight of more snow than the bracing could support. Barely awake, he yelled, "Go, Sport!"

Sport scooted out as if they had held drills for this strange exercise. The hurled sleeping bags landed on top of him and Mickey turned back to reach for the pack. Halfway out the door he was struck by broken saplings, a layer of pine boughs and what felt like a ton of snow.

He fell facing the door with both of his hands clawing toward freedom. Spongy branches cushioned him in a tightly packed sandwich where he was trapped with his head, shoulders and arms out of the collapsed shelter.

The intense pain in his back told him it was broken. The frantic dog was licking his face and Mickey managed to say before he lost consciousness, "Not dead, don't cry."

Chapter Sixteen

The bereaved doe had jumped onto the shelter roof to get revenge on Mickey for murdering her son. He could understand why a mother would do that and heard Flag laughing at his dilemma, trapped where he too would die.

Gary sighed to say, "I told you Flag would win, didn't I?" and Sport opened his wise mouth to tell them, "Nobody wins or loses. They just live and die and that's how it is."

Mickey mumbled, "You don't have to die, Sport, you can go home. Show them how far I got." They had done a lot of living since last June and he could feel Sport promising to do that.

His cheeks were already starting to freeze as he said, "Good boy." He took a careful breath to ask, "Could you bring me a sleeping bag?"

Sport tried to get the down quilt tucked around Mickey's body, but unfortunately it lay on melting snow, which wasn't too helpful. Sport began to try to dig him out with one paw and Mickey sighed; "Never mind, you're as hurt as I am. It's a good thing I put our names on the rock."

What had happened to the fire? The roof had fallen in and there had probably been enough air to support a fire. *Was the whole cage about to burst into flame around him?*

He fought his imagination; "Stupid thought. I'm more likely to freeze. What I need is a roaring fire out here."

Sport tore off to fetch firewood. He loped off-balance, his splinted paw interfering with the task, and Mickey told him, "Can't light it, don't bother."

The desperate dog didn't hear him and Mickey said, "Sport, stop. The matches are beneath me."

Sport continued to fetch wood, gathering kindling and dragging over the logs Mickey had chopped the night before. He grabbed the protrusions in his teeth and arranged the wood haphazardly, the way a child would to imitate a grownup's actions.

Trembling laughter shook Mickey at the proof of Sport's intelligence and loyalty to the end. He wet his lips to say, "Good fire," and the moisture on his mouth froze. Trying to bring his hand to his mouth caused twisting pain that made a strange vision descend.

Sport's gnashing teeth were throwing sparks to light the fire. As the flame blazed up, a short, stocky man with thick red lips and dark eyes like the fawns came skiing down the roof of the fallen shelter to stop in a flurry of snow. His black beard was frosted with white and his voice was teasing as he bent down to ask Mickey, "Did you steal my trap, young man?"

Mickey snarled at him, "Your stinking trap crushed Sport's foot!"

The jolly trapper smiled to joke, "Well now you're caught, aren't you?"

Mickey retorted, "Won't kill me, trapper. If anything could kill us, we'd have been dead ten times by now. You want to try?"

Sport would teach the trapper a lesson; he always won. Mickey gambled on their luck. "Bet you seven hundred and fifty bucks, but you'll have to dig me out to get it."

116

The square little man told him, "I don't kill people. I'm a doctor, and I heal them."

Mickey growled, "Sure, with a steel trap!"

Sport's fire was making him as warm outside as he was inside of the collapsed shelter. Michael Barnes was not going to die today, and by tomorrow he would think of something. He decided to tell the mountain dweller who said he was a doctor, "Back's broken. Roof fell in."

"Mm-hm..." The trapper was dressed in white and he disappeared for a moment before materializing again to advise an amateur, "Next time tunnel into the snowdrift at right angles to the wind and the roof will hold itself up."

"Next time I'll do that."

It occurred to Mickey that this weird scene might not be a dream, but he wouldn't have been surprised for his rescuer to turn out to be Harold Simpson's ghost. He asked, "Do you live in an igloo?"

"No." The trapper was digging Mickey out with a short-handled shovel and he took his time answering. "You will see where I live."

His energetic breath made smoke signals come from his generous lips and he looked more like a Jewish Santa Claus than any kind of a physician.

Mickey asked hopefully, "Are you a real doctor?"

"Yes." Another smoke signal rose from his mouth.

Mickey dared to hope; "Can you take care of my friend's foot?"

"One thing at a time," the trapper replied. "Your friend most emphatically commanded that I take care of you first. Give me your name please."

"Michael Karst Barnes." Mickey felt like he had stumbled into an emergency hospital after falling off his bike. He was almost sure that he was awake, but unconsciousness was a breath away. "From Overland Park, Kansas. My father is the Postmaster. Who are you?"

The trapper said, "I have a long unpronounceable name. Just call me Doctor for now."

Sport watched anxiously as the trapper carefully lifted the broken branches. His cherubic face was reminiscent of a comic book character and his voice reminded Mickey of soothing music, murmuring, "I doubt that you'll have much to say in the next few hours, Michael. I suggest that you follow my directions as well as you're able."

Mickey had to ask, "Am I your prisoner? Are you hiding from the police?" *Would their rescuer report that a lost kid had been found with a dog or take them hostage?*

"It does look that way, doesn't it?" He gave a thoughtful nod. "But actually I'm saving your life and your friend's infected foot. I need both of you at this moment in time as much as you need me. Will that explanation suffice for the present, or would you prefer to be left to work out your own problems, now that you're no longer trapped?"

He was giving Mickey a choice, which was more than Flag had ever done. The monstrous weight was gone and the fire had been rearranged so the heat reflected toward the rock enclosure. But the excruciating pain was still there and Mickey needed to know what the odds were before he made a decision that could cost him his life.

The whiteness was like an inside-out cave and he felt like he was going blind as he asked, "Is my back broken?"

The doctor replied, "I believe your back is sprained and your right ribs are cracked. If I take you to my refuge to treat you in my own way, you must agree to remain there until I release you from care."

Mickey's back felt as twisted as a hillside pine that had been struck by lightning. Sport probably needed a doctor more than he did, but there was no way of knowing what the treatment would involve and how it would end. He only knew that he could never kill another man.

He asked, "How do I know that you're a real doctor?"

118

The trapper smiled. "Ask your friend,"

Sport was looking back and forth to listen to their conversation as if it was a tennis match and Mickey objected, "Uh-uh, no fair. All he knows is you dug me out. He'll think you're a friend because of that."

"Ask Sport who unchained him from a tree."

There was only one way he could have known that Sport was chained to a tree, and as Mickey hesitated the trapper bargained, "If you will agree to assist me with my research until spring, I will prepare you to complete your journey in such a way that each day you spend on the mountain will be a memory to cherish for all your life."

His dark eyes glowed with respect and admiration as he predicted, "I expect you to live a long time, Michael Karst Barnes, because you possess a wonderfully stubborn courage and an indomitable will."

"Until spring..." Mickey was suspicious of unearned compliments and he told himself that a promise could be broken if the doctor turned out to be a crook. Lying and cheating would come easy, thanks to Flag's instruction.

He wanted to ask what month it was now and realized that the information wouldn't make spring come any sooner. He looked at Sport and decided, "Okay, it's a deal."

His jovial rescuer appeared to have come prepared to gather up a victim whose snow shelter had fallen in on him. Loading Mickey's warmly wrapped body onto a sled big enough to hold a good-sized catch, he teased, "I had hoped to take home a nice piece of meat this morning, but my traps were empty or had mysteriously disappeared. Are you comfortable, Michael?"

"Are you kidding?" Mickey reacted as he would to Flag's taunts. If he had to ride very far on the unyielding sled he might die on the way.

119

"If you don't gasp with pain or moan in anguish I'll have to find new ways to measure your discomfort." The doctor sounded pleased with his human specimen. "I think you're going to be an ideal subject for my research. You're abnormally restrained for your age, actually stoic."

Mickey said, "There's a good reason for that, mister. I'm usually called Mickey, but Michael is okay." His dad had used his given name to bring him up short, but it sounded better than the names Flag had called him.

The doctor said, "Mickey is a name for a fat-cheeked little boy, and it no longer applies." Shouldering the heavy pack, he looked like the Hunchback of Notre Dame asking, "Would you like me to give you a sedative for the trip?"

Mickey growled, "No drugs! You can cross that off your list while you're experimenting with me!"

The doctor replied calmly, "I use only natural methods. You'll never be given anything you'd find objectionable, because the side effects from your anger would negate any value to your body. I will educate you to the available methods and you will be in control of your own treatment."

He took a few cherry-sized apples from his pocket to offer, "This fruit has a mild effect on the pain center in the brain. It works quite rapidly, so you can determine the dosage. I believe that a patient would go to sleep before he could die of an overdose, but I've never overfed a subject in order to find out. I suggest that you hold a few wine apples in your hand to sample as needed for pain."

That sounded fair enough and Mickey accepted the fruit to ask, "What about Sport? He can't walk very far."

The doctor fastened his snowshoes as he replied, "We're in no hurry, and I promise not to challenge either of you beyond your endurance. We'll be home before the blizzard strikes."

Pushing the sled as if it were a baby carriage, he advised, "Don't increase your injuries with tension. Release

120

the pain by allowing your breath to rise and fall normally. The falling shelter isn't what sprained your back, Michael. You probably twisted it by lifting your pack with one hand while trying to catapult your body to freedom. Had you made a full turn to grasp your burden with both hands and then rolled backwards in a properly rounded fall, you'd have suffered no damage and been able to extricate yourself easily from the branches and snow."

"Wow, is that right?" Thanking him for those late pearls of wisdom, Mickey supposed he was right. A victim whose face was pressed to the ground had as much chance of changing his mind as a fat little kid falling into a river.

The wine apple tasted like the white wine his mother liked best, and Mickey decided to see how a small bite would affect him before giving into his desire for comfort.

A moment later, as he began to relax and the pain was leaving him, a strange thing happened. He could feel Sport's pain and tension being released along with his own.

Chapter Seventeen

The spacious, homelike cave where the doctor lived was as unlike the forbidding cave where Mickey's journey had begun as Gary's insanity had differed from Flag's. As he was helped into a firm leather hammock he wondered how much of his memory of meeting the doctor had been true. Unconsciousness and reality had overlapped like layers of falling snow, and now all he could be sure of was that an agreement had been reached, because he was here.

Exactly where was another mystery. A roundabout route through hills and over a small frozen lake, vaguely seen though the numbing wine apples, had resulted in foggy confusion. Now gentle warmth and more çomfort than Mickey had known for months was warning him not to get too relaxed. The doctor's retreat seemed like heaven compared to the places where he and Sport had slept, but it was unreal, to say the least.

The wide cavern that held the doctor's functional furnishings was illuminated by an abundance of dancing light from several kerosene lamps. It appeared that he had lived here for years, and the sight of that much luxury in the wilderness made Mickey doubt his eyes and question his brain.

He saw no scientific equipment in the cozy dwelling that contained everything else a mountain dweller might require. The doctor didn't even own a thermometer to take Sport's temperature, but whatever else this lively hermit might be, he obviously saw himself as a healer.

Sport didn't seem at all worried. He hadn't bothered to inspect their winter quarters before flopping gratefully on his side to rest. The fact that the Retriever trusted their rescuer concerned Mickey as much as it impressed him. Sport was as inclined to take new friends at face value as Gary had been, which could earn him the same reward.

Sport showed no sign of suffering when his swollen paw was lanced and drained. It didn't upset him that the eccentric medicine man used none of the sterilization procedures a city boy would expect to find in a doctor's office.

Wiping his scalpel on a rumpled rag, the doctor apologized, "I'm sorry my trap hurt you, Sportin' Life. I wasn't expecting someone of your domestic caliber to trip it. We're lucky it was only your paw. My traps are designed to break the neck of an animal biting into the bait, and a merciful death is usually instantaneous."

Mickey asked, "Do you own a gun?" He bet there was a tranquilizer gun somewhere in the cave. The leather cradle where he lay was rigged to accommodate everything from a baby raccoon to a grizzly bear.

The doctor wrapped leaves around Sport's bloody paw as he replied, "Yes, but I've never had occasion to use it."

He slipped a net stocking over the dressing to keep it in place and told the patient Retriever, "Please don't chew on that." He turned to ask Mickey, "Does he understand me?"

The dog's nose was wrinkling at the pungent smell and Mickey said, "I think so. Is it going to heal, Doctor?"

"The paw will be as good as new," he replied confidently. "And since Sport will never trigger another trap, the mishap will be worth the discomfort." Examining the scar on Sport's head he remarked, "It appears that most of his suffering was caused by a fear of helplessness, and perhaps

123

guilt that he wouldn't be able to shoulder his portion of the responsibility. You've raised a wonderfully sensitive pet, Michael. His loyalty --"

"He's not my pet." Mickey clarified that from the start. "He's not even my dog. Sportin' Life thinks I'm his responsibility. He feeds me and takes me for walks. He even disciplines me if I throw a tantrum." Something was loosening his tongue, probably the wine apples, and he stopped short of confessing that Sport had pretended to go mad to make him swim out of a cave.

The doctor smiled. "I would call the two of you remarkably fine specimens of the human and canine races."

"Useful to your research?" Mickey's eyes moved over the furnished cavern, already planning his escape, which would not be an impetuous move.

The doctor rose as he replied, "Useful to completing an education that will help me establish my practice in a new location. I intend you no harm, Michael Barnes. Before we part company I'll win your friendship, unless your spirit has been too scarred to respond to treatment."

Putting away his medical kit he cautioned, "Let me say that anger and defiance can be valuable weapons, but they will never serve you as well as the tools of knowledge and intuitive perception."

His earnest expression relaxed in a smile as he added, "But we have all winter to talk and study. You will benefit more from a peaceful night's rest than conversation." He began to extinguish the kerosene lamps although it was still early. "Nothing will bother you here. A howling blizzard can rage outside, but a bear in hibernation will not have more peace than the inhabitants of this sanctuary."

He sounded like a minister offering a blessing as he promised, "In the spring you and I will proceed to our separate destinations more ready to face what the future holds because of having known each other. Goodnight, Michael;

goodnight, Sport." The last lamp flickered out and Sport yawned noisily in the darkness.

"Goodnight..." Mickey's reply seemed to hover in the air above him. Staring at nothingness, he told himself it wouldn't hurt to be polite as long as he never let down his guard. The way his rescuer kept repeating that there was nothing to be afraid of increased Mickey's suspicion that there was a sneaky catch to his hospitality.

What did the doctor mean by saying that his spirit had been scarred?

***

"Some physicians believe that immobility is the best treatment for a sprain." The doctor began Mickey's instruction the next morning after a breakfast of 'weed soup' that contained a combination of plants that grew locally.

"Others argue that the problems arising from immobility, such as stiffness, weakness and constipation, aren't worth the added time it takes to heal injured ligaments. Then of course, there's boredom. Do you suffer from boredom when you're inactive?"

He began to work on a piece of leather he was tanning and Mickey had the feeling that the doctor wasn't the kind of person who could sit around and be social for long.

"I don't know." Mickey confessed to not knowing himself that well. "I used to read comic books or watch TV for hours. That would probably bore me now, but I'm not anxious to go mountain climbing. Do you own a radio?"

It seemed like the doctor should have heard about a missing boy and a Retriever, even in this remote sanctuary.

"Yes, but the battery ran out a year or so ago." The doctor reached for a large needle and threaded it with a narrow strip of leather as he said, "I regret that we can't have music, but I have a wealth of reading material. Do you enjoy reading, Michael?"

125

"Not really…" Except for comics, Mickey's reading had been limited to homework. "Unless you've got a book on how to use the stars for a compass."

"Yes, I do have that, as well as many excellent texts on survival." The doctor's dark eyes lit up and he hurried to a floor-to-ceiling bookshelf that could have been built by a cave dweller.

Mickey asked, "Do you mean survival in the mountains?" All those books had to have been transported to this remote location by something like a helicopter and he thought about the pilot who had ignored his frantic signals.

"Every volume on my shelves relates to survival." The doctor brought Mickey three books as he said, "I regard Shakespeare as vital to the starving intellect, but we'll satisfy your thirst for knowledge before introducing wisdom."

Eagerly studying the worn texts, Mickey wasn't surprised by how interesting the Boy Scout Manual had become since he left home. The fact that he was gaining knowledge that would make it possible for him to find his way home gave him new hope, and at dinner the next night his host teased, "For one who doesn't enjoy reading, you certainly have taken to it."

"That's not reading; that's self-defense." Mickey dug hungrily into a combination of tastes that were new to him.

"Nicely stated," the doctor laughed. "But is not culture a useful defense against a lack of self-respect?"

Mickey said wryly, "If you're looking for intellectual conversation you dug out the wrong greenhorn."

"I think not." The doctor's reply was serene. "Forgive my scientific curiosity, Michael, but were you born with a wiry toughness or is that quality a result of recent events?"

A bite of marinated venison stopped in midair on its way to Mickey's mouth and he had to laugh. "It's so recent that I hadn't noticed it. Are you kidding me?"

"I'm perfectly sincere. Can you tell me what makes you so suspicious?"

Mickey counter-attacked; "What's your name and why are you here?"

"Ah, yes," the doctor nodded. "All right, we will both keep our secrets." He refilled the dish Sport had licked clean before he said, "But you need to realize something, my friend. Treating the body for a wrenched back and malnutrition is not enough. Whole health depends on --"

Mickey interrupted, "Malnutrition? We had enough to eat." But never like this feast of soup and salad and stewed meat. "We would have been fine if it hadn't been for your miserable trap and the stupid roof falling in."

His host informed him, "You would have died from eating too much lean meat and a lack of proper air circulation. Your skin tone, your fingernails and your irritability tell me that before another month had passed you would have suffered from headaches with dizziness as well as digestive difficulties. I'm sorry to say that dauntless courage is not enough, Michael. I respect and admire you both -- I'm amazed by your ability to learn from nature, but you were never equipped for this hard life, were you?"

"No, I wasn't." Mickey had diagnosed those symptoms as general nervousness and he glared at his fingernails, wondering how they told the doctor so much.

"Astonishing." The doctor leaned forward in his chair to ask, "Can you tell me how long you've been alone? That is, the two of you. For my case history, that's all."

"About six months." It felt like six years.

"Really... And your age?"

"I was fifteen in July." *Unimportant information; the doctor already knew his name.* "You can see that I wasn't a blond." The roots of his shaggy hair were brown as a bears and Mickey had to add, "I didn't do that. Someone thought it would be funny and I couldn't undo it."

He had been a pale towhead until he was seven years old and he had stopped wearing baseball caps when his hair finally began to darken as his mom had promised it would.

The doctor sighed. "I'm sorry you were mistreated. We can change your hair color if you like, but I wouldn't advise cutting it until spring."

"I'm not looking for sympathy." Mickey's dad had always cut his hair and he wanted to wait until he got home.

"Then I shall offer none." The doctor smiled at the Retriever who had come to sit between them when his hunger was satisfied. "I invited Sport to join me when I unchained him from the tree, but after thanking me for his freedom and a meal, he hurried off in search of you."

Mickey said, "We're in your debt. Tell me about your work and how you want us to help you." He decided that it would be a mistake to get used to eating well. Learning how to stay healthy was more important.

The doctor gathered up the dishes as he said, "There's no hurry. I need to decide how to describe that to you. Conversation is a new pleasure for me, Michael, and since we have a mutual need to close the door on the past, our relationship must be built with care. Please ask for help if you need assistance turning over during the night. This is important to your healing."

Mickey agreed, "All right, I'll call you."

The doctor appeared to be a compassionate man. Sport trusted him completely, but it was becoming more obvious by the minute that this scholarly, slightly mad natural healer was looking for more than pleasant companionship in his remote research laboratory in the Rocky Mountains.

128

Chapter Eighteen

"When I was a small lad, not even in school yet, I became aware of my calling to heal. I gathered patients wherever I could find them. Birds, insects, animals, and occasionally people."

The doctor was changing the dressing on Sport's paw as he told Mickey, "My grandmother said the gift was in my hands. My father laughed when she said I had healed a burn for her before it could blister. Grandmother told me I should never listen to doubters, because healing is a God-given talent that isn't dependent on book-learning."

Mickey lay in the hammock listening to every word and trying to decide if the doctor was lying or hiding something. Sport was watching Mickey in the same way, probably reading his mind.

"When I was in fifth grade I treated a friend who had fallen from a tree. His leg appeared to have been broken, but the X-rays showed only a crack that hadn't separated. Father carried on something ferocious about how we could have been sued and his salary attached for life because of my reckless audacity.

"After that I made people swear to secrecy before I would help them. It became a neighborhood joke how I signed up for every First Aid class, but each instructor taught me something new. The more I studied, the more I grasped, although I was frequently confused."

"What do you mean?" Mickey sensed confusion now.

The doctor sighed. "Medical books and teachers were foolishly sure of themselves. My intuition often argued that their statements were wrong or incomplete. But of course education in itself can be a disease..."

"How so?" That sounded pretty crazy to Mickey.

The doctor frowned, looking for words. "It's like this, Michael. A teacher can introduce a wrong thought like a germ. Education can feed the error with more misinformation and students may embrace a concept that's false, or so incomplete that it's invalid."

Sport looked bored enough to chase his tail and Mickey had to admit, "You're losing me. Could you put that in plain everyday language?"

Flag had brainwashed Gary into thinking society was sick, and nobody was going to do that to Michael Barnes.

"It's this way." The doctor sat down to look into Mickey's eyes and his tone became stern. "The knowledge that comes from any book must be weighed and proven by the student who will use it. You must test and question those who teach you, for to know something is of no earthly value until you must use it. Do you see?"

"Well, sure." Mickey shrugged to agree, "That's only common sense."

The doctor warned, "Many times in education, teachers will pass on something they were taught that was never proven to them. Educators seldom deal in common sense. Think about this: how would you like to be taught to build a shelter by someone who never had a need to stay safe and warm? Someone who had never braved the wilderness."

"I get your point." Mickey realized that the doctor was as much of a fanatic about healing as Flag had been about

130

crime, but his message made sense, especially the part about questioning so-called experts.

He continued, "This made me decide that schooling, medical schooling in my case, was incomplete. Even those who practiced what they preached subscribed to a law of averages and focused all their attention on the flesh. Listen, Michael; sick patients, whether animal or human, are individuals whose flesh is supported by mentality. They're highly subject to emotion, and modern medicine refuses to acknowledge that man is by nature spiritual! If we do not treat his spirit, or at least recognize it, then a physician will heal one illness and the patient will turn and catch another."

"So what method do you use?" Mickey wondered how he and Sport figured into all of that.

"We're coming to that." The doctor's smile returned but emotional undercurrents still vibrated in the cave.

"To put it in a nutshell: at an early age I found the power of healing in my hands. My parents were afraid of that power because they were more educated than Grandmother. In high school my healing ability was ridiculed as spiritualism, or superstitious myth.

"Oh the names I was called." The doctor's head shook at the cruelty of youth. "During my internship I came to distrust my gift, and by the time I started to practice medicine I was substituting conventional methods for intuitive ones. It was too important at that time of my life to have patients and be respected."

"But now you're doing it your way?" Mickey suspected that he had been found guilty of malpractice or worse. Suddenly the leather hammock felt too comfortable and he needed to sit up in a chair.

The doctor helped him make the move. "Now I'm going back to school. Nature's school." His hand gestured to take in the mountain and all its creatures. "I'm sorting out what I learned from teachers, experience and intuition so I can treat patients from the inside out."

"Hmm…" That sounded to Mickey like the treatment might include nosy procedures like hypnosis.

"Don't misunderstand me, Michael. Case histories and statistics aren't harmful unless they're applied without regard. So here I am, learning how to use the most natural methods I can find within a few miles of my primitive laboratory. Whenever possible, I put my patients' wellness into their own hands and make it their responsibility."

The doctor stood in front of his bookshelves to declare, "For I believe what will keep a man from getting sick is independence, self-respect, and a sense of security. What will protect him from injury is tested knowledge, an even temper and patience with nature. What I want most of all to teach is this. Know thyself, heal thyself.

"My method, therefore," he summed up his lecture; "is to exercise my intuition plus my education, using what nature has provided in the wilderness. Civilization has much to offer, my friend, but civilization can dull the mentality and interfere with intuition. Sport has taught you that during your months in the wilderness, has he not?"

Mickey said, "Yes, he has. I've been teaching myself that, I think. The hard way." His mentality had definitely been dull and he had confused intuition with impulse.

Now he realized that his education had no value in this place. He needed to learn how to keep himself and Sport alive, and he was reminded of his prayer in the cave. *'God, I promise to learn everything I need to know.'*

That was probably what made him an ideal subject for research, and he inquired with a new respect, "Can you tell me how long you plan to stay here?"

"I'll stay for one more year. I have had seven now." The doctor teased him, "You're wondering why I'm so well equipped when there's no road to my retreat. The answer is

132

simple, but it's someone else's secret and I would need permission to share it."

He went to brew some herb tea as he said, "When I return to society I'll be a physician in an institution where the rules are different from those in a city hospital. My patients will know their spirit is the sickest part of them, and those who are waiting for death will not be forced to suffer a living hell."

"You mean a lunatic asylum?"

"Have you ever known anyone who was insane?"

"Yes." Pain twisted in Mickey's chest.

Gary might have had a chance for a normal life if Flag had been taken to a doctor who could heal his anger. Mickey looked at Sport to see what he thought, but the disinterested dog had fallen asleep, and he could only say, "I still don't understand how you want us to help you."

The doctor explained, "My patients here have been everything from a bear suffering from a terminal blood disease to a beaver in need of dentistry. Sportin' Life is my first domestic animal and you're giving me the opportunity to use intellectual devices I couldn't suggest to an animal."

He glanced at the bookshelf to add, "But perhaps if you were to read Shakespeare aloud to Sport, his sensitivity to your reaction would add to my data. Tell me, Michael, do you find me insane?"

"A little... Yes and no." Mickey was honest. "I never heard anyone talk like you do. Maybe you're eccentric. That's what my mom calls people my dad calls nuts." He laughed to confess, "I've wondered about my own sanity a couple of times." *More than a couple of times.*

"May I ask about your parents?" The doctor handed him a cup of tea.

"I'd rather you didn't." Homesickness rolled over Mickey like a breaking wave.

"Just this then. Are they living?"

133

"Yes." Mickey stared into the teacup. "Good people."

"I see... Then your present dilemma is not related to an unhappy home life."

"No! My back is sprained, not my mind!"

Hot anger flashed and Mickey guessed that his spirit was also out of whack. "Listen, my only problem is I was never prepared to be a mountaineer. As far as my spirit is concerned, I went to Sunday school every week like clockwork, but I'm not -- well, religious. I believe in God, I'm almost sure about that."

"Do you believe in yourself?"

"More than I used to." Mickey was embarrassed and he changed the subject. "I believe in Sport for sure. I thought he must be immortal when he was able to track me after he had been chained to a tree."

The answer to that mystery was so simple. Sport had been unchained. "Listen, Doctor, did you ever --"

Mickey had to stop for a sip of tea before he could ask, "Did you ever meet anyone who felt like they had died and woke up afterwards?"

"Oh, yes." The doctor's dark eyes glowed. "And their stories are quite similar. I would be curious to hear yours."

"What was the same?" Mickey couldn't begin to describe his experience.

"I have my notes on that somewhere." Setting down his teacup, the doctor went to get a book and open it to a marker. "Yes, here we are, fascinating data! In almost every case the subject felt himself being pulled along a warm tunnel and there was a light --"

Mickey whispered, "What was that?" He straightened up too fast and the pain made him hold his breath.

Sport raised his head as if he heard a noise outside. Then he came to peer into Mickey's face.

The doctor said, "That's all right, Sport, it's only a growing pain. Michael, blow your breath out to release

134

your tension. Stretch your heels; then let your toes slowly drop. Close your eyes to take another breath; blow it all out and open your eyes with a softer focus. Only receive the message with your mind. Now let's see..."

He read from the book; "'The bright light at the end of the warm tunnel draws the subject to a personage of great kindness and comfort.'"

"That's amazing..." Mickey tensed and he repeated the exercise that worked almost as well as wine apples.

The doctor turned a page to read another passage. "'When the subjects were drawn back to life they experienced a sense of regret, or perhaps loneliness. Then they felt a deeper gratitude for life, or increased bitterness because of helplessness and pain.'"

"Wow..." Mickey's eyes met Sport's and they both wondered. "I thought it was only --"

"A dream? I think not, Michael. I think dying is like that." The doctor refilled their teacups as he said, "I believe that after the tunnel and the kind person there is a heaven, but not as man has designed in his immature writings."

He chuckled at the rich imagination of man, then he sobered to state, "But I am convinced of the spirit's immortality. If I did not believe with all my heart that the spirit is immortal, I would stay here for the rest of my life and treat the innocent patients I can find within a day's journey of this natural wilderness."

Chapter Nineteen

Weeks passed. Mickey read the doctor's books on mountaineering and learned to tan leather. He found out how to create needles and thread from natural materials and he made some leather moccasins. After finishing Chuck's snakeskin belt he made a leather watchband to replace the expanding metal band that had gotten uncomfortably tight.

Sport's paw healed and Mickey's back mended. His husky voice gained a deeper resonance and only cracked under occasional tension. He had grown into the clothes Flag had given him and his nightmares were less frequent.

His wise therapist assigned tasks that had practical value and watched for an opportunity to introduce studies of a cultural nature. One night when Mickey reached for the dictionary he suggested, "Try the thesaurus."

"Who?" Mickey laughed at the unfamiliar word. "Sounds like a prehistoric book."

Sport's tail wagged at the welcome sound of his laughter and the doctor smiled to say, "It's the dark blue book with the tattered binding. You might find synonyms fun, and an adequate vocabulary is self-defense."

Flipping through the pages of the thick thesaurus Mickey was doubtful. "I can understand why it would help to identify plants by name, but Sport and I get along better

136

when I don't use a lot of words." Their communication had become almost telepathic since he had stopped using the dog for an excuse to talk to himself.

The doctor remarked, "You might find yourself in a place where the right word at the right time could make the difference between a reward or a beating; imprisonment or freedom. Is this skill not related to survival?"

Mickey had been in that place, and the small print in the book blurred as he argued, "Big words won't help."

Jokes and stubborn guts was what had saved his skin. *Animal instinct*, he realized now, and he wasn't proud of having killed two men. Flag had hesitated to pull the trigger, and that instant of uncertainty had cost him his life.

The book came into slow focus and Mickey saw the word *Stupid*. Scanning the long list of words under that heading, the one that seemed to describe his actions was *foolish*. He had been foolish, not stupid.

Reading on, he decided that he had been more ignorant than foolish. Chuck apparently suffered from a limited vocabulary; Dumb-bell wasn't even in the book.

The doctor took some meat out of his old-fashioned icebox as he agreed, "Small words are best as a rule, but making conversation with strangers will never intimidate you if you polish your language skills. If a man knows three things he can hold his own with any antagonist he will ever meet."

"Name them." Mickey reached for a pencil.

The doctor got out his carving knife and cutting board before he answered, "The art of self-defense, the confident use of language, and the power of directed emotion. If you're secure in these practices you can face a howling mob and conduct it like an orchestra."

He sharpened the knife as he added, "On the other hand, display uncertainty, show fear, be awkward in verbal response and people will use you to their advantage."

137

Mickey was writing as fast as he could and he said, "You're going too fast."

The doctor gave his attention to cutting the meat for a moment. Then he said, "A secret treasure of words -- combined with the wisdom to know when to be silent -- will assure you of serving no god but your own. Then you'll be able to face any human situation with a smile."

He waited for Mickey to finish writing before he drove the message home. "Should you find yourself testifying in a court of law, would it not be a comfort to know that a thousand words are at your disposal to present your case?"

Mickey said, "That's a strong argument, counselor."

Gary's security had come from quoting his big brother, and it had collapsed like a poorly built snow shelter when Flag turned out to be a loser.

***

Roget's Thesaurus proved to be fascinating reading when a person had nothing better to do than play with words. There were a lot of choices in the categories that most concerned a fifteen-year-old who was uncertain of his crime. Even if Flag and Gary's death was a clear-cut case of self-defense, Michael Barnes could be accused of hunting out of season, cutting saplings in a national forest and driving a vehicle without a license. He had probably done things he didn't even know were against the law.

As the doctor had promised, a basic knowledge of Latin and Greek roots made the biggest mouthfuls in the English language easy to figure out, and learning the origin of words simplified adding them to his vocabulary.

Mickey had always preferred Monopoly to Scrabble, but the game was a pleasant way to pass the time when his opponent wasn't out to make him look illiterate. Reminded of how playing poker could reveal a man's character, he asked his host, "Could you teach me to play chess?"

138

"I would love to do that." The doctor beamed with pleasure confiding, "Living alone, what I've missed more than anything else is playing chess."

At supper that night Mickey looked at the meat on his plate and knew it would choke him if he tried to swallow it. The vegetables tasted delicious, but the sight of the rare meat reminded him of the soulful eyes of the fawn he had killed more than a month ago.

He couldn't imagine why that should bother him now, and when the watchful doctor offered to cook the meat a little longer he said, "Don't bother. Maybe I'll become a vegetarian now that I know it's possible."

The forest was rich in edible plants, and when he got home he would plant a vegetable garden so his family could learn to appreciate fresh greens.

The doctor warned, "I can't advise that at this time. A good deal of strength and energy is derived from eating meat, as long as you balance rabbit with fatter meats."

Mickey supposed that his delayed reaction was related to watching the doctor sharpen and wield the carving knife. He figured that the problem would pass, like every other obstacle he and Sport had managed to overcome.

After supper he gave his attention to learning the properties of wood. That came under the heading of self-defense for sure, because fire was a basic necessity and having a proper shelter was as important as a balanced diet.

By the next evening he was able to name all the wood samples the doctor had collected. He memorized them in order of their heat generating properties. Hickory, beech, birches and hard maples were valuable foods as well. The second group included ash, elm, locust, and cherry. Birch bark would flare up even in water.

Spruce, pine balsam and fir twigs were filled with resin and burned like torches. The heavier a wood was, the more heat it would throw, and green wood could be mixed with dry woods to create a long-lasting fire that would guarantee a full night's sleep.

His teacher complimented him; "You're an apt student, Michael, more hungry now for books than for meat. Did you do well in school?"

Mickey had to laugh. "Not at all. I never had a reason to study until now."

He was learning a basic navigation system so he could use the stars at night to plot his course. He would never admit to anyone that he had thought that moss grew on the south side of trees! Except Sport, of course, who had made a few mistakes of his own.

He failed to find any reason for studying Shakespeare. It put Sport to sleep every time, maybe because the words flowed like a rippling stream that ended in a waterfall. Putting Shakespeare aside, he stalled by asking the doctor, "You said I was your only human guinea pig. Does that mean nobody else was ever here?"

Nature didn't provide things like brass lamps, hooked rugs and foam mattresses. They had to have come by air.

The doctor replied, "A friend drops by occasionally, but since he's never ill I couldn't call him a patient. Without his kind counsel I would not have adjusted so readily to this isolated retreat."

"A hermit?" Mickey pictured a scraggly-bearded old coot chewing tobacco and dressed in smelly animal furs.

"Of sorts." the doctor chuckled at the word. He began to mend the binding on the worn thesaurus as he said, "My friend is a forest ranger. He loves the natural wilderness as much as the comfort of civilization, and cherishes his solitude as much as being with his family."

Mickey steeled himself to ask, "What's his name?"

140

"Blaine Kern. His visits have made the brightest days in my years and I hope you'll have an opportunity to meet him before you leave in the spring."

Sport's whimper sounded like he was mourning the dead ranger and Mickey cautioned, "Shh, Sport, no one's coming." A wave of guilt broke over him as he explained, "Sport associates rangers with being chained to a tree."

"But why would…"

The doctor's voice faded as Mickey turned away to keep from having to answer questions.

Silence filled the cave. Sport looked from Mickey's face to the doctor's and he scratched at an imaginary flea.

Mickey decided, "I'm going to bed now if that's okay. I've done all I can for one day."

He couldn't tell the doctor how Blaine had brightened his nights and shadowed his days ever since an ignorant hostage had blown his cover to get him brutally murdered.

The nightmare that sucked Mickey into a whirlpool of images seemed worse than drowning or being lost in a cave. Suffocating smoke was coming from a campfire by a deep green pool and he could hardly breathe.

Gary shrieked like a bobcat when Mickey began to fight Flag for the gun and Sport came running through the trees to leap on Flag. The gun discharged and Flag threw the dying dog into the fire. Gary couldn't stop screaming when Flag forced Mickey to eat the charred meat.

Flag made Gary choke down enough tranquilizers to kill him, and then Sport floated up from the fire and began to bark, telling Mickey that it was only a dream.

The doctor's voice commanded, "Wake up, Michael! Open your eyes and look at me. Don't twist about like that; you'll injure yourself."

Sport's front paws on the hammock were making it rock and Mickey opened his eyes. Seeing the doctor's sympathetic expression in the lamplight made him bury his face in the dog's fur to hide his tears.

"Let nature have its way." The doctor encouraged him to cry. "Tears aren't a sign of weakness but of sensitivity."

Mickey choked, "We're not going to make it home. I'm too tired to go anywhere." He felt like he had stored his tears for a year, not daring to let himself cry for fear that he would never be able to stop.

The doctor spoke soothingly. "Realize that you're back in control and no danger threatens us here. Sport will not be afraid unless you are. Focus on the flame in the lamp and rest... Be at peace, Michael, and let reason return."

The flame was a tiny campfire warming his face and then his body. He asked, "Am I sick? Do I have a fever?"

The doctor told him, "You're suffering from fear. Nightmares come from an unreasonable dread, or some traumatic reality we've never faced in the light of day. Could you talk about it?"

"That won't help." *Flag was dead and buried, but he was still winning.*

Sport uttered a piercing bark that made Mickey wince, and the doctor said firmly, "If you cannot let go of this evil demon that claims your dreams, you must chain it to a tree. It must not be allowed to have its way with you."

Mickey begged, "How can I fight it? It comes when I'm asleep, and I never know it's a dream until I wake up."

The doctor repeated quietly, "Look at the lamplight to release your tension. Breathe deeply and let yourself feel more and more relaxed with every breath. Sport is here and you're safe in the peaceful, warm flame. Rest, Michael... release the fearful images and see only the truth of this moment... Relax and let yourself sleep."

Mickey didn't want to go back to sleep; he was afraid that Flag might be waiting, but the doctor's melodious

142

voice repeating reassuring phrases made him admit, "I died in the river and woke up in a cave."

"And before you were in the river?"

"Fishing… with Dad and Chuck. I can't get this stupid lifejacket fastened! I've gotta stand up for just a minute--"

Sport whined and nudged Mickey with his nose.

Mickey scolded him, "Will you get out' my way, you big floor mop? Oh God, no! I'm under the river!"

"Five, four, three, two, one…. Wake up now, Michael. This tragedy is out in the open where you can look at the truth of it and start to live with the facts."

Mickey's tongue crept out of a sleepy mouth to wet his lips and he cleared his throat to say gratefully, "Longest dream I ever had in my life." It was over at last, and he knew that wouldn't happen again.

"Hypnosis, Michael." The doctor apologized, "I fully intended to discuss this treatment with you first, but your need was desperate and you were ripe for psychotherapy."

"Ripe?" Mickey didn't understand. "For hypnosis?"

"It seemed best not to interrupt you when your thoughts began to flow so freely." The doctor's red-rimmed eyes were puffy from crying for a murdered friend and he cleared his throat to say, "You welcomed the treatment, you realize."

"You hypnotized me?" Mickey realized that he had just revealed everything he had planned to keep secret. "You tricked me!"

"I lanced an infection in your spirit," the doctor replied stubbornly. "I drained the poison from a festering wound in your mind."

"Bullshit! You betrayed me!"

The doctor took a cautious step backward and his smile was uncertain. "I can't promise that the wound won't leave

143

a scar, but we've eliminated the possibility of amputation. Your spirit is intact, I'm glad to say."

"*Confession under duress,* that's what you did!" Mickey had learned the legal term just in time to use it.

"I exercised a physician's prerogative, Michael, and a doctor is under oath never to reveal anything a patient --"

"Do you still have a license to practice medicine?" Mickey cornered him furiously. "I don't even know your name, is that fair? You know everything I've done, everything I feel! You promised I'd be in charge of my own treatment, but all you wanted was a human guinea pig! I have no bargain with you now, Doctor, and this time there's two against one!"

"I was afraid you might see it that way, but it was a risk I had to take." The doctor asked him quietly, "Do you realize how unwise it would be for you to leave now? Or were you thinking of making me go instead?"

Mickey snapped, "I'm not a murderer!"

Neither of them could go anywhere. Winter would kill anyone who tried to find his way out of the mountains.

"I know that, Michael," the doctor said. "I'm not concerned for my life. I'm only saddened by the cruelty that forced a boy into manhood before a gentle adolescence could bridge the chasm. I don't need to analyze you to know that you're remarkably able to adjust to circumstances. Your ability to cope with one shock after another gives me hope for your generation, and your friendship --"

"It's not for sale!"

"That makes me proud indeed." The doctor lit another lamp as he said, "It helps me make a difficult decision."

Mickey stormed, "You're crazy! Dammit, Sport, how could you sit there and let that happen?"

He was furious with both of them, and then he remembered that Sport had tried to warn him. His breath blew out and he comforted the worried dog, "Never mind, I'm the one who talks too much. What decision?"

The doctor said humbly, "You've made me realize that if I can't trust a man of your caliber I'll never have a friend in the world, and that's a dim outlook indeed."

"Oh, yes, I agree." Mickey was deliberately sarcastic. "Very dim."

"So the time has come for me to tell you about myself. My name is Solomon Montelani." The sound of his own name made the doctor wince as if he expected Mickey to explode again, and he said, "If you don't wish to bear any more responsibility than knowing that --"

Mickey growled, "You confuse the hell out of me! What responsibility?"

Solomon Montelani went to unlock a cabinet by his bed as he said, "To know the secrets of another can become a heavy burden. I shared your burden because it was breaking your heart, and what you've told me will follow me to my grave unless you require my testimony at an inquest. Then I'll help you as much as I'm able."

He took a small strongbox out of the cabinet to say, "Likewise, what I reveal to you now must be kept secret until I take up my residence in prison."

Mickey was heartsick repeating, "Prison..." *God, was everyone in the mountains a criminal?* He shook his head to say, "Don't tell me; all I want to know is whether you're a lying murderer."

"That was the debatable issue," the doctor sighed. "The legal limitations of a doctor's --"

"Malpractice, I knew it! Spare me the gory details." Mickey closed his eyes and Sport nosed at his hand to keep him from going to sleep again.

Solomon stated with dignity, "There are no gory details. I simply allowed nature to run its course by refusing to keep patients in a living hell."

Mercy killing. Mickey had to ask, "How many people?" Had Dr. Montelani ended one patient's suffering or a whole hospital full of people?

"Two people..." He was having trouble getting his strongbox open and he frowned to correct himself; "No, three, but no one ever knew about the first. I was caught red-handed the third time short-circuiting the works. Witnesses to that event recalled similar circumstances regarding the demise of another patient of mine a year earlier, when the electrical system apparently failed."

"Jesus..." Unable to find him guilty or innocent, Mickey needed to hear the rest. "What about the one they never knew about?"

"The first patient I trusted to nature's mercy, fourteen years earlier, was my son. He had been brain-dead for months and I'm sure that hastened his mother's passing. Mercifully, she went to her heavenly reward unaided."

Mickey was reserving judgment as he asked, "What's in the strongbox?"

"Newspaper clippings," Solomon said. "To assure you that I can't blackmail you without retaliation."

Mickey informed him bitterly, "What I did to Flag and Gary doesn't hurt as much as what I let them do to me."

"I understand." Solomon gave a slow nod. "A man's dignity is his only God-given possession." He gave Mickey the clippings as he said, "In fact, that was my rationale."

"But I did kill them." Mickey wept, confessing, "It was my fault that Flag killed Blaine. God, I'm so sorry!"

Solomon said, "That is your belief. Let me tell you mine. You'd have given your life to keep Flag Chasen from murdering Blaine. And it's not likely that you would have attacked Flag in a rage if he hadn't tried to kill Sport.

"Flag's actions were in character with his nature. He was programming you to be violent, and your reaction was a result of that conditioning. The fact that Flag was afraid

146

to kill you was his undoing, and Gary's reaction to his brother's death was totally predictable. Your instinct to survive ended that tragic series of events in the way nature decreed. You were the most worthy to multiply your seed."

Mickey knew that Sport would agree, but he would need to think about that. He handed back the newspaper clippings without reading them because he was unwilling to subject himself to the conflicting opinions of journalists.

Solomon promised as he turned down the lamps, "By the time we part company in the spring you and Sport will be more than prepared to find your way home. I predict that you will also be prepared to enjoy more happiness than most men ever find in a lifetime."

"Probably…" Mickey guessed he was right about that.

Solomon said in the darkness, "Oh, Michael, you and Sport give me such faith in the future of this planet."

Chapter Twenty

Mickey told Sport, "That's enough wood for now. The fire will last until morning. How do you like our classy shelter?" He bragged about his finished effort. "I bet it'll still be here the next time we come this way."

Sport looked over the sturdy little shelter and wagged his tail to agree that his partner was pretty smart.

"Yeah..." Mickey took in a deep breath of fresh spring air. "We're learning everything we need to know."

New life vibrated with energy all around them and he felt wonderful as he put the cooking pot over the fire and gathered browse to make a bed of fragrant pine. There were fresh greens for supper with venison jerky and herb tea.

Sport sniffed at the bed and his eyes were teasing.

Mickey warned, "You lift your leg on that, son, and you're dead meat."

He pulled off his heavy boots to inspect his feet for blisters or chaffed places before putting on his comfortable moccasins. Maintaining his health was doubly important when he was out on his own and he knew that giving daily attention to his feet would insure being able to travel.

His clothes were starting to collect body oils that would keep his pores from breathing and make him lose body heat. Tomorrow they would find water so he could bathe and do the laundry. When the stars came out tonight he would make sure that the short-cut Sport had insisted on taking hadn't thrown them off course. Then he would draw today's hike on the map to show where they were in relation to their final destination.

This wasn't Mickey and Sport's first solo trek since Solomon had begun assigning mountaineering exercises. Hours had been spent hunting game and searching out plants with nutritious or medicinal value. Mickey had built a snow shelter a ten-minute hike from home, slept in it during a blizzard and cooked several meals for himself and Sport. As Solomon had predicted, that exercise had ended the nightmares about the shelter that collapsed.

The doctor had documented the extraordinary communication that had developed between Mickey and the Golden Retriever, noting that while it wasn't uncommon for a canine companion to exhibit telepathy, humans were rarely able to respond in kind.

The winter months had been put to good use. Mickey had learned seven ways to light a fire, countless methods of shelter building, and he was fairly good at predicting the weather. His pack was lighter than before but contained every tool that was essential to survival. He could pack it in six minutes, almost as fast as Solomon. He was equipped to hole up and wait for rescue as most experts advised, or to walk out under his own power, which only a veteran mountaineer should undertake.

He had sewn his suede pants and jacket from a pattern Solomon had helped him make. He wore loose fabrics next to his skin to retain heat and allow air circulation as well as for comfort. The jeans he had outgrown had become a patchwork vest and Solomon had supplied the material for two pullover shirts.

The boots Flag had given him had been stuffed to make them fit, but at the rate he was growing they would be tight by summer. Then he would need to stand in shallow water and hike his boots dry to keep them broken in for a comfortable fit.

Using a fire-stick to light a gumwood campfire that would show Solomon where they were, Mickey's sense of security was reinforced by knowing that a triangle of fires with three smoke columns would alert forest rangers that a traveler was in trouble.

Solomon had taught him the eleven body positions for signaling aviators as well as how to use a mirror to send Morse Code, and now he knew why his wild waving on Dinosaur Ridge had been ignored. The pilot was on his way to drop supplies to Solomon and couldn't risk being questioned about his interesting cargo. Not getting a clear distress signal, he had written a note telling Solomon to watch for a dog and a youthful traveler who might need help.

It would take a serious setback to make Mickey signal for help. The town of Miracle Falls was only seventy miles away and he agreed with Solomon that making this solo trek was essential to his independence and self-respect.

When they had parted company three days ago, Solomon had remarked, "Nice weather for a walk," as if Mickey's final journey was only one more exercise.

Replying, "Yes, it is," Mickey had found it impossible to say goodbye to the friend who had become his mentor.

They would meet again, if not next spring, then in Solomon's new location. The thought of visiting him in a top-security prison didn't repulse Mickey or fill him with dread. He knew that the men there would be as different as their crimes. They would need Solomon as much as he had -- especially any who had been declared guilty through a miscarriage of justice. Solomon would heal all who would let him and document criminology in a new light.

Sport whined and came to lie close beside Mickey, missing Solomon too, and Mickey gave his back a rub as he asked, "How're you doing? Ready for supper?"

Sport reflected his warm contentment. He was ready for anything, and Mickey said, "What do you want to bet that we'll miss the peaceful beauty of the mountains?"

Sport knew they couldn't come back until after they had gone home and Mickey told him, "Maybe we'll need to balance our cushy lifestyle at home with living in the forest, the way Blaine did. I should make the marker now so we won't have to do that before we leave in the morning."

He had been surprised to learn that leaving one's name at campsites was advised in all the books on survival. Grown men had been known to perish an hour's walk from their campsite, simply for lack of knowledge about the abundance of nature. Solomon believed that Mickey's optimism in the face of misfortune had kept him alive, which supported his theory that the health of the spirit came first.

They slept soundly after supper, with Sport rousing only twice to utter sharp warnings to potential marauders.

When morning came Mickey sat on a log to reach for the soft leather pants that provided the best protection against poisonous insects. At that vulnerable moment a cantankerous scorpion chose to challenge the optimism of Michael Barnes and he gasped in pain as the stinger discharged venom into the back of his bare knee.

Sport crouched to attack the invisible enemy that had attacked his partner and Mickey quickly crushed the scorpion with a rock before Sport could be stung.

Grabbing his leather belt to make a tourniquet, his fury erupted in every cuss word he had learned from Flag. Then he told the worried dog as he applied a suction cup to the swelling, "Don't panic, I know how to use a lymph constrictor and I won't faint at the sight of the blood when I

151

use the scalpel." He knew he wasn't going to die of the poison, it would only feel that way.

Sport whined, feeling helpless in this new crisis, and Mickey gave him something to do. "Fetch some wood for a triangle fire in case we need to call for help. I'll set up a dew-catcher to take care of the water detail."

He had learned enough about anatomy to know that he had been stung in a sensitive area. Getting out the mirror to operate on the back of his knee, Mickey was determined not to light the triangle fires unless he felt that his life was threatened. Forest rangers could show up at the same time Solomon arrived, and he doubted if they would share Blaine Kern's compassion for an escaped mercy killer.

The main problem was whether he would know if he was dying, and he told the listening dog, "That decision might be up to you, partner." If the signal fire became necessary, Sport would find a way to light it.

As soon as the messy surgery was over Mickey set up the dew catcher and added his blood type to his name on the marker. His hand was starting to shake as he wrote,

Stung by a scorpion enroute to Miracle Falls
Final destination, Overland Park, Kansas

Chapter Twenty-one

Miracle Falls looked like a town that had overslept. Winter had overstayed its welcome and spring was tiptoeing in as if reluctant to disturb an unpredictable ogre.

Solomon had told Mickey that only the hardiest souls stayed in Miracle Falls during the winter and the tiny town became almost as deserted as the ruins of Snakesville.

The post office at the east end of town hadn't opened for business yet although it was late April. Mickey peered through the window at a 'Wanted' poster near the counter and saw Flag and Gary's picture among those of the outlaws. Their faces seemed to stand out, perhaps because Flag was wearing a friendly smile and Gary looked angelically handsome.

Then Mickey realized it was because he had become intimately acquainted with the Chasen brothers. He was glad to see that Solomon's picture wasn't on the poster. After seven years the local police had apparently decided that Dr. Montelani was someone else's problem.

There was, however, a two-column news photo of a round-faced kid named Mickey Barnes. That picture had been taken for his Junior High graduation and he had to laugh quoting Solomon; 'Mickey is a name for a fat-cheeked little boy.'

He opened the unlocked door and stuck his head in to call, "Hello? Is anybody here?" He waited a moment, then stepped in and called again, louder, "Hello?"

Sport sat by the door to wait, as any well-mannered dog would, and Mickey told him, "Come with me. Something about this doesn't feel right."

Walking to the bulletin board to read the article with his picture, he remembered Flag joking about the fact that two other people had mysteriously vanished from the same area. Then Sport growled a warning and he looked up to see a hard-faced lawman's bulky frame in the doorway.

The sheriff's hand lay on his gun as he demanded in gravelly tones, "What're you doin' in here?"

Sport took a stiff-legged stance between the gun and his partner as Mickey replied, "I wanted to buy some stamps. The door was open and I called out first." He would have bought stamps if anyone had been selling them.

"Standing wide open, huh?" The sheriff's reply was heavy with sarcasm but he was eyeing Sport with respect.

"I mean unlocked." The importance of the right word hit Mickey full-blast and he added, "When I found out that no one was here I stayed long enough to read this article."

Showing the sheriff the clipping, he felt an instinctive distrust of the first member of civilization he had met upon his return. "You can see that the door hasn't been forced."

"Don't get cute with me!" Miracle Falls' sheriff was more suspicious than the occasion called for, demanding, "What's your name?"

"Michael Barnes." Mickey handed him the clipping as proof of his identity.

"Dammit, that's not funny, and I'm not amused!" The sheriff glowered at him to snap an order. "Let's you and me go across the street. And you keep that mean lookin' animal under control or I'm impounding him!"

154

Mickey cautioned Sport not to overreact as he told the fidgety lawman, "He doesn't like your tone of voice." He had pictured his triumphant return in a dozen ways, but it had never occurred to him that he wouldn't be believed!

He asked the sheriff, "Have you had a lot of trouble around here?" It wasn't easy to maintain a casual tone as he crossed the street. The way the lawman was crowding him from behind was an insult to human dignity, and Sport was walking almost sideways to keep his eye on the gun.

The sheriff's answer was a frustrated growl. "This place is a hot-bed of trouble! People around these parts are very nervous, so you'd better watch your step. Where were you planning to go with that backpack?"

He sounded like a Chicago gangster impersonating a western sheriff and Mickey decided to tell him, "I've already been."

A grizzled old resident who had emerged from a coffee shop sneered at Mickey as if he and Sport were vagrants. Then he grinned at the sheriff to tease him, "I see you're hard at work earning your keep, Sheriff Burnside."

Burnside grunted, "Mornin', Ben. Open the door."

"You bet." Ben kept a watchful eye on Mickey as he obeyed and got quickly out of the way.

Mickey found the sheriff's office as small and cluttered as his mind. The furniture looked like rejects from an antique store, and someone had written *clean me* in the dust on a filing case in the corner.

The sheriff closed the door before he rasped, "Winter's no time to backpack in this territory. What happened to your leg?" Still holding the gun, he seemed to find Mickey's limp further proof of juvenile delinquency.

Mickey replied, "A scorpion up on the ridge didn't like my looks any better than you do. I'm not carrying any identification, but I think my parents will know me."

No one else would recognize him from that faded news photo. His face matched a lithe body that stood five foot ten, and his shoulder-length hair was darker than when he had left home. Mickey's gaze was level with the sheriff's and his voice had deepened, but he felt sure that his mother would know he was the sunny-faced kid who had been lost at Pinecrest almost a year ago.

Burnside's mouth twitched and his words exploded with fury. "If you think I'm gonna call those poor people and make 'em come all the way up here to be disappointed again, you've gotta different think coming! I oughta' slap you in jail for defamation of the dead!"

Mickey was almost sure there was no such charge and he asked, "What do you mean 'disappointed again?'"

Sheriff Burnside snapped, "I mean claiming to be Mickey Barnes has gotten to be a damn popular sport!"

Sport objected to hearing his name spat out like that and the sheriff jumped behind his desk to threaten Mickey, "You watch him now!"

Mickey cautioned the dog, "Take it easy." He asked the lawman, "Are you saying that other people have walked out of the mountains claiming to be me?" He was sure he wasn't dreaming; his fever had broken five days ago.

"You're the second one, mister. The first screwball is still locked up." Burnside's splotchy face revealed the ravages of his responsibility saying, "Charlie Barnes had a stroke when this bogus Mickey turned out to be a teenaged loony. I'm never gonna bother those good people again. Let some other cop take the rap!"

"Oh god…" Mickey was sick inside, picturing the only stroke victim he had ever seen -- a sixth grade teacher who had died a week after his paralyzing seizure.

"God, indeed." The frustrated sheriff demanded, "Do you have any idea of the hell families go through when a beloved child disappears off the face of the earth? Natalie

Fields' father still comes up here and wanders around like a ghost, searching for signs of his daughter, after seven years. Bert Carson's son lives in fear that his drunken father might come back some night, and God only knows how Tom Morgan's orphaned kids will manage." His tight voice broke adding, "If Blaine Kern doesn't show up pretty soon, this town will never believe in miracles again."

Mickey said emptily, "You forgot Harold Simpson."

"Who?" The sheriff flinched. "Who did I forget?"

"I found a skeleton in a cave north of here. Harold Simpson, October 9, 1932."

Mickey could clear up a lot of mysteries for the sheriff if he would stop making accusations long enough to listen. "Did Natalie Fields drown? Was she --"

"Listen, tough guy," Burnside interrupted angrily. "The last kid who walked in here pretending to be Mickey Barnes got a free ride to a loony bin. That was last Thanksgiving, and it'll be a snowy day in July before I'll listen to tall tales from some transient teenager who breaks into the post office! That fifteen-year-old was suffering from exposure. He had no reason to want to be himself, but all you've got going for you is an alleged cave and a scorpion." His head shook with disgust. "And a skeleton named --?"

"Harold Simpson." Mickey steeled himself to ask, "How bad off is my fa -- Charlie Barnes?"

The sheriff sagged into his decrepit leather chair. "When Mickey's family flew out here to identify a nutcase it was the last straw for them. Poor old Charlie was struck down right where you're standing, and that sweet little mother would have been a widow by now if young Chuck hadn't kept his head and known how to keep his dad alive until the paramedics showed up."

"I had no idea..." Mickey had pictured his family safe at home, warm and comfortable, and he realized that his homecoming was going to be very different from the way

157

he had pictured it. He told the sheriff, "I don't blame you for being upset. I didn't come here to add to your troubles."

He started for the door, needing to revise his plan, and the sheriff barked, "Hold it right there! I want to know exactly what you and your hunting hound have been up to. What's your name, and why are you in Miracle Falls?"

Sport was looking up at Mickey to see what he would do now, and he could only say, "I'm Michael Karst Barnes from Overland Park, Kansas. I've been lost in the Rockies for eleven months, and when I finally found my way to Miracle Falls I decided to report to the ranger station here since Pinecrest was closed."

"How did you know it was closed?" Burnside's eyes narrowed. "Did you read it in the newspaper, the way you found out about a lost kid? How old are you, mister?"

"Five weeks short of sixteen." Mickey didn't try to remind him that boys grew up and became men. "I sympathize with your problem, Sheriff. When you find out that I'm telling the truth you're going to feel worse than you do now. The trouble is you're asking the wrong questions."

"*Damn!* Are you tryin' to tell me how to do my job?"

Mickey said evenly, "No sir, I'm not going to tell you anything at all, because it's obvious that whatever I could say would only make you sicker. I'm going to leave now, because I haven't done anything to be held for and I don't want to cause you any further embarrassment."

Burnside dialed the phone as he snapped, "You're not goin' anywhere, sonny! I'm shipping you to Kansas City so you can answer to the juvenile authorities there. Isn't that what you want, to go home?"

"What about Sport?" Mickey felt like running for the woods and Sport tensed, urging him to obey his intuition.

"He'll be shipped on the same plane, tranquilized out of his mind." The edgy sheriff spoke rapidly on the phone;

158

"We've got another Mickey Barnes on our hands, and this time I'm -- *Hey!*"

He dropped the phone to yell, "You come back here! Stop those two! Don't let them get away!"

Mickey's backpack made escape difficult and his limp slowed him down, but the ranger who darted out of the coffee shop wasn't ready for hard action. Sport sprang at him to knock him down and Mickey kicked him in the stomach when he tried to roll back up. By the time he could recover from the double attack they were passing the post office.

As soon as they reached the cover of the woods Mickey dropped the pack to the ground and told Sport, "Head for the water and lead them away from me."

As he hid the pack in the undergrowth he could hear a jumble of orders being shouted not far behind. Then Sport's bark called '*this way, this way.*'

The sheriff's shout sounded like an echo, commanding, "That way, men!"

A moment later, perched high in a tree with his knee throbbing painfully, Mickey could see five men pursuing the racing Golden Retriever. He was aware that resisting arrest made them look guilty of the sheriff's accusations, but being shipped to a Kansas City juvenile facility with Sportin' Life crated and tranquilized was not the way they had planned to go home.

Chapter Twenty-two

An article about Mickey and Sport appeared on the front page of a local newspaper that served a triangle of towns below Miracle Falls. The article wasn't the headline feature -- that had to do with a town meeting regarding prayer in the schools -- but it was right below that hot controversy where no one could possibly miss it.

'*A tall youth claiming to be the missing Mickey Barnes was escorted to the Miracle Falls Sheriff's office at gunpoint this morning after he broke into the Post Office and took a year-old clipping from the bulletin board. The backpacking teenager stated that he had been living in a cave where he was stung by a scorpion. Refusing Sheriff Burnside's offer to be flown to Kansas City, the youth and his dog escaped into the woods after viciously attacking the police officer who ordered them to halt.*

'*The imposter is six feet tall, approximately eighteen years old, has dark brown hair and eyes and was wearing imitation leather clothes. The dog is a mixed-breed German Shepherd and Spaniel. Both are considered dangerous, and if seen should be reported to the local authorities.*'

The photo that accompanied the article was captioned, '*The real Mickey Barnes who drowned at Pinecrest.*'

Mickey left town without bothering to find out the name of the place. Even if he wasn't eighteen or six feet tall, he and Sport were still arrows pointing to each other.

He camouflaged a lean-to in the woods and told Sport as they ate the last of the venison jerky, "The final leg of our trip might be as hazardous as the first. We're not going home tranquilized or in handcuffs."

He put the article with the one he had taken from the post office as he said, "Solomon was right about not believing everything you read. Come here, you mean-looking Spaniel, we'll have to keep each other warm tonight. We're outlaws now and building a fire is out of the question."

His first order of business would be to buy some clothes that would let him fade into the crowd. But the only cash he had was in fifty-dollar bills, and if he tried to spend them wearing his 'imitation leather clothes' he could be labeled a thief as well as an imposter.

Wondering what Solomon would advise, he told himself, "Use your imagination, Michael."

The solution turned out to be so simple that the hardest part would be to keep a straight face. He decided to stroll into a Cheyenne tourist trap that featured western apparel. Then his cash would talk so loud that the salesperson wouldn't see anything else.

It was the kind of nervy plan Flag would have applauded. Sport waited in a shadowed alley across the busy street and Mickey was more worried about being separated from his partner than he was about being spotted by a cop.

He swaggered into the exclusive boutique and the swishy clerk greeted him; "That's a stunning outfit you're wearing! All handmade, isn't it?"

Mickey's bored eyes looked past the clerk as he said, "The Navajos do this work in Arizona, but I picked it up in the south of France."

His sneer imitated Flag's lazy grin as he said, "I have a closet full of unique clothes and I'm tired of playing the life of the party. Show me something that's the current fad without a lot of decoration. Keep it in the hundreds if you can, because my broker refuses to advance my allowance and the bank will take back my Lincoln Continental if my payment is late again."

He moved unhurriedly but didn't waste a second. A blue denim suit with two pairs of pants and three cotton shirts cost three hundred and forty dollars. Mickey's roll of fifties didn't surprise the clerk who only suggested putting his purchase on a credit card so he could keep his cash.

Mickey confessed with a grimace, "I ran up a three-thousand dollar tab last month and I'm trying to discipline myself. As long as I don't get mugged I'll be all right."

The clerk folded Mickey's clothes to put them in a box as he remarked, "You might have been taken for a Mickey Barnes impersonator in this handmade suede outfit, although it's obviously authentic. All you'd need is the tough-looking dog."

Mickey asked, "Who? I thought I knew everyone on American television." Hearing his name drop as if he were world-famous made him breathless.

The chatty clerk explained, "People have been disappearing in the mountains north of here and it's made quite a stir. Even the national news takes note when five people vanish into thin air."

"I guess..." Mickey wanted to say that a double layer of tissue paper wrapping wasn't necessary, but he drawled, "I seldom watch the news. Who's Ricky Burns?"

"That's Mickey Barnes," the clerk corrected him. "He's a Kansas City boy who was lost during his summer vacation -- drowned, to all appearances. A kid who insisted he was Mickey got everyone all excited last November, but he turned out to be an unhinged orphan looking for a family.

Then a few days ago an ill-mannered backpacker claiming to be Mickey Barnes started the rumors flying again."

Mickey said, "Some guys will do anything for attention. Would you break another couple of fifties for me? I need to pick up some cigarettes before I have a nicotine fit."

"They'll catch up with him, don't worry." The clerk counted out ten-dollar bills as he said, "He's traveling with a big ugly dog and his outfit wasn't honest suede any more than he's the real Mickey."

Mickey couldn't help remarking on his way to the door, "Wouldn't it be ironic if the kid turned out to be on the level? A year is a long time."

"No chance," the clerk replied. "Chuck Barnes told the press that the tough kid the sheriff described couldn't possibly be his little brother. He said his Retriever would never have attacked a cop and Mickey would have welcomed the opportunity for a free ride home." He sighed sadly to add, "Listen, if Mickey Barnes were to walk through that door, even I would recognize him by his pug-nosed smile."

Mickey's smile died and he said, "I've been wondering where to go to break the monotony. Maybe there's some excitement left at Mystery Falls."

"That's Miracle Falls, sir, and I wouldn't advise it." The sober clerk warned, "Most tourists are afraid to venture beyond Rocky Vale these days."

"They aren't as bored as I am." Memorizing the name of the town they had left in a hurry, Mickey drawled, "I've got time to kill and nothing better to do."

***

A Cheyenne newspaper that carried Chuck's disclaimer ended with a direct quote:

This latest pretender's actions are completely out of character for my brother, and that dog can't be the Golden Retriever I raised from a pup. There isn't one real scrap of

163

evidence to give us new hope, and my only prayer is that imposters who stir up trouble will get what they deserve.'

Mickey was grateful to Solomon for telling him that crying was a sign of sensitivity, not of weakness. The fact that Chuck had become the family spokesman confirmed that he had become the man of the house, and he was obviously trying to keep a painful wound from being reopened.

Mickey knew it wouldn't do any good to call home. Unless his mom recognized his voice she would call Chuck to the phone. He would give Mickey hell for impersonating a lost child and then everyone would cry.

Fresh tears fell as he said, "I think of myself as being the same, but I'm not! Solomon was right. The only way to get past Mickey and the pug-nosed smile is to stay independent and keep our self-respect. That means we're going to have to finish this whole trip without asking anyone for help."

Public transportation was out unless Sport could pretend to be a Seeing Eye dog. If he tried to rent a car he would have to show an ID, and not many people would pick up a longhaired hitchhiker with a large dog. It seemed like no matter what they did they would be risking arrest.

Mickey's nose wrinkled and he felt of it. All of him had grown longer than he had been a year ago, even his nose. He bet it would have taken two years for him to grow that much if his dad had let him stay at home to watch TV and read comics. He might never have progressed beyond a seventh grade level in language skills, and he certainly wouldn't have learned to appreciate Shakespeare.

He smiled remembering his brother's disgust when he packed his comic books for the dreaded vacation. Then Chuck had sunk to the floor laughing when Mickey yelled, "I'll give up listening to my comic books when you stop reading your stupid rock and roll music!"

Chuck had agreed as soon as he could stop laughing, "That's a deal, Mick."

164

Now Mickey slumped in despair to moan, "We can't go home. We can't suddenly reappear, for god's sake, coming back from the grave. They think we're dead, and Dad could have a heart attack if we walked in there without any warning. They're not going to believe it, even when they see us in the flesh. The trouble is I'm not Mom's little boy any more. Dumb little Mickey was lost in the Rocky Mountains and there's nothing I can do about that."

Sport nosed at his hand and Mickey saw that his lean, strong hand was that of a man, not a child. He mused, "My fingerprints would be on file if I had ever been arrested."

He saw that his watch had stopped, as if his childhood were past history, and he muttered, "All I've got to prove I'm me is a watch with a dead battery and a beaded belt anyone could have found in the woods."

Sport whined, echoing his frustration, and Mickey took in a deep breath to tell him, "This calls for patience, my friend. We could be home by tomorrow night, but the family needs time to prepare for the shock."

A new fear struck and he whispered, "God, what if they've changed as much as we have?"

***

Mickey called his family doctor from a public phone booth during the noon hour. Dr. Harkness often answered the phone himself when his receptionist was away from the office and Mickey was relieved to hear him say, "This is Doctor Harkness."

"Did I catch you at lunch, Doctor?" Mickey pictured him opening a carton of milk and tossing a crumpled Butterfinger wrapper in his wastebasket.

Dr. Harkness said, "More or less; what's the problem?"

He sounded like he hadn't changed and Mickey said, "My health is fine, but I'm caught between a rock and a hard place." His dad's pet saying fit the situation to a T.

165

Dr. Harkness kidded, "Need bail?"

Mickey said with a laugh, "No sir. I just need you to talk to someone for me. I heard that Charlie Barnes had a stroke and I'm worried about the rumor that another weird kid is running around pretending to be his missing son."

"We're all worried about that." The doctor's friendliness cooled. "Who is this?"

"This is Mickey." He sped up to deliver his prepared speech. "Listen, I have a diamond-shaped scar on my right hip from where Hodge broke a pop bottle on me and I almost blew my left eye out on the Fourth of July when I looked in a knothole to see why the firecracker hadn't gone off. You took out my tonsils when I was eight and I made you save them in a jar. Mom's maiden name is Turley and I called you Dr. Barkness when I was little. What else can I say to make you believe me?"

After an anxious moment Dr. Harkness said, "*Mickey*? Where the devil are you?"

"I'm on my way home, but after everything that's happened, I'm afraid to walk in on my family without any warning. I thought maybe you and Reverend Hasty --"

"But where have you been all this time?"

Dr. Harkness had heard a hundred boys' voices change and it was easy for Mickey to tell him, "Lost, that's all -- until I finally made it back to Miracle Falls with Sportin' Life, who is not vicious! We're just tired of being kicked around. Can you understand that?"

"Of course, Mickey. How can I help you?"

A police siren was wailing somewhere in the distance; Mickey couldn't tell whether it was closing in on him or over the phone. The city noise was making him nervous enough to explode and he told the doctor, "My family has been through hell this year and I'm hoping that you and Reverend Hasty can soften the shock of my homecoming."

166

Bitterness crept into his voice as he added, "I'm sending that misguided sheriff a letter answering the questions he should have asked me instead of accusing me of breaking into his unlocked post office. I'm mailing my Scout belt to Reverend Hasty at the Methodist Church because our troop met there and he razzed me about running out of room for my name. With luck, we'll avoid any more panic. I need to call Chuck's best friend to ask for his help. Would you say Dan Carlin --"

"Yes, I would. Do you need his phone number, son?" Papers rattled as the doctor fumbled through the clutter on his desk to find a phone book. "Mickey, could you tell me the name of your fourth grade teacher? Not for myself, but in case someone inquires if I asked you any questions."

"Danny's mom, Mrs. Carlin." Glad to be able to answer an intelligent question, Mickey told him, "After her was Mr. Pierce. Sixth grade was 'Evil-eye' Eiken who got re-tired for smacking Lillian Merch in her receding chin. You told me in secret that Lillian probably asked for it."

"Now I'm sure of it." The doctor laughed with delight. "Here's Dan's number, but don't inquire about his mother's health. Martha died with very little warning in January and Dan despises being alone."

Mickey sighed. "I'm sorry to hear that." He wrote the number the doctor gave him and asked, "If we come home on Friday will that be enough time to get them ready?"

"Don't wait any longer than that." The doctor cleared his throat to say, "I want to see you myself. A lot of people would very much like to see you. You say you're healthy?"

"I've never been so healthy in my life." Mickey couldn't help bragging, "I got stabbed by a scorpion a while back, but considering that he got me in the knee joint the leg is hardly sore at all. Sport had a fit watching me operate on it, but I must have gotten the poison out because I'm not dead.

Hey, don't tell Mom about the scorpion. When I had Chicken Pox she was afraid I'd be permanently scarred."

He was chattering almost like he had at fourteen and the doctor asked huskily, "Do you remember what you said about that, Mickey?"

"Something about a dot-to-dot game…"

"That's exactly right! Oh, Mickey, I'm so glad you're alive and safe. I feel like I must be dreaming."

Mickey told him, "I'm going to call back in an hour to remind you of your appointment with the Barnes family."

Dr. Harkness promised, "My secretary will tell you that I've already left to keep that appointment. This is the most rewarding emergency call I will ever make."

***

Danny Carlin's reaction was the exact opposite of the doctor's. When Mickey said, "I'm calling because you're a friend of Chuck Barnes," he snarled furiously, "Who says?"

It sounded like they had become bitter enemies and Mickey asked, "You're not?"

Danny replied nastily, "Chuck and I were best friends until he took advantage of that to steal my girl! So what's your angle?"

"Excuse the ring; sorry I bothered you." Mickey guessed that girls must have become very important to Chuck and Danny if a passing romance could destroy a friendship of eleven years.

Danny demanded, "Did Allison tell you to call me?"

Mickey said, "No, and I'm calling long distance, so I'll spend my money on some other friend if you'll give me a clue. What about Steve Monahan?"

"Long distance?" Danny repeated uncertainly. "Is Chuck in some kind of trouble?"

Mickey had to laugh. "You're mad at him, remember? Do you want him in trouble?"

"No! What's this all about anyway?"

"It's about his brother."

Danny's anger did an about-face. "You mean Mickey?"

"Does that make Allison less important?"

"Who is this? Why did you call me?"

"Because Chuck's about to be put to a serious test of nerves and he'll need a good friend standing by."

Danny said, "Hey, how much rougher can it get? Listen; is this about the weirdo who showed up in Miracle Falls last week? What do you know about that?"

Danny's wrath focused on the impostor and Mickey bet that it had started with the shock of his mother's death.

"I know how to handle it," he said calmly. "It's very simple, Dan, but I need you to ask Chuck to send Sheriff Burnside a sample of Mickey's handwriting. I'm sure they've kept something besides old photographs. A handwriting expert will be able to nail a phony, isn't that right?"

"Man, that'll fix that rotten --"

"And if he's not a phony," Mickey interrupted, "Sport and I will be able to come home with dignity instead of being shipped caged and tranquilized to Juvenile Hall."

"Is *that* what they was going to do...?" Danny sounded appalled, and then he stuttered, "Hey, is this -- I mean, are you really --"

Mickey repeated, "Send his handwriting to Sheriff Burnside, Dan, and if you need to talk someone, touch bases with Reverend Hasty or Dr. Harkness instead of blowing your mouth off to the press. They know what's happening."

"They do?" Dan was breathless, agreeing, "Well, okay, I'll get right on it."

Mickey ordered, "And go easy on Chuck, because this has nothing to do with your girl problems. If you discuss my phone call with anybody who starts an uproar, I'll sick my vicious dog on you."

169

"Ease off, man." Danny's laugh was forced. "I can keep my cool."

Mickey had wanted to talk to Danny Carlin this way since he was nine years old and he enjoyed saying, "Just remember that you weren't a six foot three basketball whiz when you were a pimply fourteen. You grew up, and hopefully got smarter."

Danny said soberly, "I'm calling Chuck as soon as you hang up. If this turns out to be a con-job you won't have to sick your dog on me. Your brother will kill me. I must be crazy to even listen to you."

Mickey said warmly, "Thanks, Dan, I appreciate it."

His letter to Sheriff Burnside was rewritten five times to get the words right before he registered and mailed it, making sure that Chuck would get the return receipt.

'Sheriff Burnside, I appreciate your protecting my family and I sincerely regret our misunderstanding. I left your office in a hurry because the way you wanted to send me and Sport home was lacking in dignity. It would have embarrassed a lot of people, including you.

'I called my brother's friend Dan Carlin and told him to have Chuck send you some of Mickey's handwriting. My writing may have grown up with my body, but I'm sure that a handwriting analyst can compare it with this letter and give you an expert opinion. With luck, the samples might also provide some fingerprints. (See mine below)

'By now you may have found Harold Simpson's name in your missing persons file. (Oct. 9, 1932) You will find his remains about a hundred feet from where a stream pours out of the mountain near Miracle Falls. There's a deep hole north of two waterways that create a small triangular island. The opening is about twelve feet round and drops down into the cave system. Don't try to use the rotten rope there or you may end up like Harold. (No humor intended.)

170

'You will find my name and the date I was there near Harold Simpson's. The reason my bones aren't there is because Sport made me crawl through a small tunnel leading to the pool where the river flows out.

'We got out three or four days after the undertow in the river above Pinecrest pulled both of us into the cave. Then we had to climb the mountain because there was no other way. I was in no shape to find my way back to Pinecrest after that, even if I had known how.

'I was fuzzyheaded for weeks and didn't develop any confidence in myself as a mountaineer until we survived the winter. I would have died a hundred times if it hadn't been for Sport, and I saved his skin two or three times.

'Sport was not my only companion on the mountain. Death and my guardian angel were within hailing distance most of the time, but neither of them communicated like Sport. If you'll try to imagine what we've been through you'll know why I can't treat Sport like an ordinary dog.

'You and I weren't prepared to meet on that day. We were both oversensitive and we weren't acting intelligently. When we meet again I know that things will be different.

'I phoned my family doctor, Gerald Harkness, and our minister, Reverend Bill Hasty. They live in Overland Park and they're both satisfied that I'm the same Mickey Barnes who vanished last June. I've asked them to prepare my parents for the shock of my homecoming.

'Please inform Dr. Harkness as soon as my handwriting has been verified. We plan to arrive home on Friday afternoon unless there's another hang-up. After waiting this long, getting it right is more important than anything else.

'Thanks for helping me clear up one of your mysteries. A thorough search of the cave could solve others.

'Yours truly, Michael Karst Barnes.'

171

When he mailed the letter at the post office he saw the Chasen brothers' picture among the wanted criminals. Sport was waiting for him across the street, peering into a bike shop window as if he was an interested customer, and Mickey started to call, "Let's go."

Then he went to see what the dog found so interesting. All he saw was a bunch of new and used bicycles. The message sunk in slowly and he said, "Duh, why didn't I think of that?"

Sport sat on the sidewalk to wait for Mickey to buy them a bike. After the sale was completed Mickey told him, "I may be slow, but I catch up. I hope the same can be said for you when I get myself and our pack on this hot bike."

All they had to do now was decide where to hide until people stopped calling them imposters. As a dirty name, Mickey preferred Dumb-bell.

Chapter Twenty-three

Mickey chose the University at Fort Collins, Colorado as a logical place to hole up and wait for the seeds he had planted to germinate. Chuck had called the college campus small enough to be homey and Mickey figured that one more male body merging with the masses wouldn't be noticed, especially during final exams.

As he parked his bike in a rack he wondered if he had made a mistake. He tried to tell himself the more people the better but the cozy campus seemed to have become a teeming city and Sport was reflecting his uneasiness.

It was reassuring to see male students who were shorter than he was and had longer hair, but being eyed by pretty coeds unbalanced him. Hoping that the college crowd in Colorado was less intrigued by the Mickey Barnes myth than the populace of Wyoming, he decided that lying on the grass with a book on his chest would make him look like anyone else who preferred napping in the fresh air to claustrophobic dormitories.

He thought about studying forestry in college and wondered if his folks could afford to send him here. His dad might be on a skimpy pension since the debilitating stroke, in which case it would be necessary to earn a scholarship to supplement his college insurance.

A plastic Frisbee sliced across his shoulder to interrupt his daydreaming. He nearly caught it by reflex before it rolled off to lie on the ground, and he murmured to Sport, "Relax, we're not being attacked."

"Hey, man, I'm sorry about that." A short student whose round glasses were bent out of shape apologized, "Did we get you in the face?"

"It's okay," Mickey smiled at him. "I'm unbreakable."

The friendly student laughed. "You sure woke up in a hurry. You almost snagged it in your hand. You must be a champ at this."

"Just a fast reactor." Mickey hadn't thrown a Frisbee for over a year and he had never been good at catching it.

The Frisbee player's partner called, "I'll see you later, Jess. I need to pay a library fine and check the Ride Board."

Jess waved to answer, "Let me know if anyone's going to Albuquerque." He reached over to give Sport a friendly rub as if he had a dog of his own at home.

Sport blinked with surprise, but he didn't growl at such familiarity the way he might have a week ago. He was re-adjusting to civilization faster than his cautious partner.

Mickey said, "I don't suppose you know anybody who's driving to Kansas City." He wondered where the Ride Board was and if it was only available to students.

"Hey, you're from KC?" Jess told him, "My roommate lives there, but he took off after the frat bash. He should have waited for a sober driver." Laughing at his reckless roommate, he advised, "Check the board in the Commons, you'll probably find someone going in that direction."

"Do you think they would object to Furry Face?" Mickey explained Sport's presence. "I seem to have been adopted, and I'm too burned-out to argue."

Jess grinned. "He looks like a really nice dog. You're a purebred Golden Retriever, aren't you?"

174

Sport appreciated being addressed like a visible equal and he offered his paw to a new friend.

Jess laughed and said, "Man, cozy up to a girl like that and she might detour to Kansas City. Women are fools for dogs." He confided, "That's why I'm becoming a vet."

A bulletin board in the Commons was crammed with cards stating whether students were looking for a ride home or passengers to share expenses. Mickey found a card that said *'Kansas City, leaving ASAP'* and took it off the board to hurry to the nearest phone.

After several rings a sleepy voice mumbled, "Oh, that's Jeannie. She's at the Reg; you can catch her there."

"Did you say 'the Reg'?" Mickey asked before the voice could hang up and go back to bed.

"She works at The Regulator. Just ask for Jean, okay?"

The Regulator was a bar on Main Street. There were so many young customers pushing through the swinging door that Mickey wasn't worried about the small sign that said *'You must be twenty-one to enter.'*

He apologized to Sport, "Sorry, you'll have to wait outside," and the dog went to sit in front of a drug store where he could keep an eye on the door.

Loud music was blaring and a cloud of cigarette smoke burned Mickey's nostrils as he entered. Students were talking without listening to each other and washing down thick sandwiches with beer. Mickey shouted to get the attention of a passing waitress, "I'm looking for Jean."

"You got her. What for?" She barely glanced at him and swept a tip in her pocket.

He told her, "I need a ride for myself and a friend to KC. I'll pay his expenses. He's a dog."

Jean cleared the table as she said, "I'm allergic to dogs. Dandruff, y' know? They've all got it so don't tell me how

175

clean your dog is. Anyway it's gotta be a girl. I don't dig guys, even if they're cute. I told my cuckoo roommate to say girl on our card; but if you want anything done right you have to do it yourself, y' know?"

"I know..." Mickey wanted out of The Regulator. "Thanks, anyway. I'll change the card and put it back."

"Just a minute, cutie," she stopped him. "I know somebody who needs a driver. That is, this girl I know told me her boyfriend is looking for someone to drive to KC."

Mickey suggested, "Give me the phone number and I'll check it out if you don't have time." He had never expected to be called 'cutie' and he wondered if he would be asked to show a driver's license.

Jean said, "In five minutes I'll have time. Sit down. You want a beer?"

Mickey shook his head. "Not really. Do you think this guy would object to a dog?" Being accepted as a member of the college crowd felt very strange after not being a member of anything for so long.

"All we can do is ask." A smile softened Jean's face and she advised, "Stay by the door if you're not ordering anything, and try not to get crushed by the mob."

Mickey obeyed, feeling more unstrung by the minute. He was a nervous wreck by the time Jean whizzed up to say breathlessly; "You're all set. Go to the Lincoln Theater, the stage entrance, y'know? The guy with the car doesn't care if you have an alligator. Go now, because he's on his way."

Mickey said, "That's great!" *They were home free!* "Wait a minute, what's his name?"

Jean admitted, "I forgot to ask. But you can't miss him because it's a brand new station wagon, loaded to the max."

A bartender roared, "Jeannie, this isn't a tea party!"

She yelled, "I'm coming!" and muttered, "Macho fool." She winked at Mickey to say, "Have a safe trip."

"I will. Thanks a lot." Mickey slipped her a tip.

176

Jean looked at it and gasped, "My god, I can retire!"

Mickey had intended to give her five dollars, but her astonished joy was worth fifty dollars, so he waved like a millionaire and headed for fresh air.

He felt like a millionaire until he discovered that Sport was gone. Panic set in and he tried to tell himself that it was the roar of the cars and too many people, things that wouldn't have bothered him a year ago.

A familiar bark across the street brought instant relief. He wasn't sure why the Golden Retriever had moved, but he respected Sport's reason and appreciated the way he let his partner know where he was.

He headed for his bike as he whispered, "Good boy! Now let's go find the Lincoln Theater."

***

Mickey found out that the Lincoln Repertory Theater was one of five theaters on the campus. It was located on a narrow side street at the south edge of the campus, and the only car in sight was parked in the alley by the stage door.

It was a beautiful white Chrysler station wagon. Two guys climbed out of the car when Mickey wheeled up on his bike with Sport running alongside.

The tall driver had black, scraggly hair and a full beard. His chubby passenger's head was shaved. Sport didn't like their looks any better than Mickey did, and he couldn't understand why they would need another driver.

The bearded guy asked him, "How soon can you leave?"

Mickey thought fast and decided, "Any time."

The kid with the shaved head said, "Okay, dream-boat, it's all yours." He tossed Mickey the car keys and told him, "Tank's full now, but you'll have to buy your own gas the rest of the way. Can you handle that?"

"Sure... You mean you're not going?" Mickey hid his relief. The luxurious station wagon had an automatic

177

transmission and they could sleep in the back if he left the bicycle behind.

The Beard said generously, "We're just sending you and your alligator. Leave the wheels at Seventh and Wheeler. You know where that is?"

"That's my hometown." Mickey was sure he could find it. "Where do you want me to take the keys?"

"Leave 'em under the front seat on the passenger side." Skinhead explained, "It's a surprise for my cousin Joe. His place is hell to find and he's never home anyway. Have a trippy-trip, baby."

"I will. Have a nice bike." Mickey lifted off his pack.

The Beard laughed. "Sure thing. Don't stop 'til you're off campus, because there's no student-parking sticker. If a cop nails you for any reason you're on your own. Dig it?"

"I understand." Mickey accepted the terms and opened the door for Sport.

The new car smell was making Sport hesitate and Mickey coaxed him, "Come on, alligator, let's go. Destination Seventh and Wheeler, Kansas City."

It didn't occur to him that the car might be stolen until ten minutes later, when they were flying down a clear road for home. Sure enough, when he stopped to look in the glove compartment for the registration, there was none.

He was running a stolen vehicle across the state line.

Mickey shook his head and muttered, "Crazy… I've got no driver's license, a hot car to deliver, and I can't even point to Cousin Joe. Can't you just hear Chuck saying 'You'll never learn, will you, Mick?'"

Sport sniffed at the glove compartment as if he wanted to take another look and Mickey told him, "There's only a complicated manual in three languages. So should we dump the car before we get picked up? *Dammit-all*, how come comfort always has to be so dangerous?" He was sure

178

that Skinhead and the Beard wouldn't have forgotten the registration and he was forced to admit that they had been as honest with him as crooks were capable of being.

"Well, hell, Michael, think!" He sighed to release his trapped breath and decided, "No, first rest, and then think."

He hadn't had a good night's sleep since there had been no peaceful place to build a shelter and a campfire. The wilderness had once seemed a threat, but now shopping malls and motels made him want to run for the hills.

It was really illuminating the way comfort and security depended on familiarity with one's surroundings.

***

Mickey knew it was silly to feel like they had to replenish their water supply when all he had to do was turn on a faucet. But tap water tasted terrible and Solomon would have agreed that bottled spring water was better insurance against getting sick -- especially when a hundred viruses might threaten a person who hadn't been exposed to them for nearly a year.

Thinking about water reminded him that his denim suit was starting to look slept in. The tag recommended dry cleaning and Mickey was willing to risk wearing his 'imitation leather' for an hour to protect his investment in an expensive designer suit.

He found a one-hour dry cleaner and the gray-haired man behind the counter commended him, "You're smart not to throw this suit in a washing machine. The grass stain might not come out, and it would never look new again."

Mickey said self-consciously, "The only time I plan to wear it is for church or dating. The current craze seems to be impersonating a mountaineer, but that won't last."

"It never does," the man agreed. "Your suit will be ready by four. Paying in advance will speed picking it up."

Sport was waiting across the street and Mickey asked, "Want to come with me to get the water or stay in the car?"

Sport didn't want him making the risky trek alone and Mickey agreed, "Okay, but keep a safe distance between us and don't lose your cool if people stare at me."

His rabbit fur moccasins, leather pants and patchwork vest were attracting attention, but now they were miles from Wyoming and mystic legends of people who vanished into thin air.

There was a Sparkletts dispensing machine between a hardware store and a Safeway market. Sport pretended to be waiting for someone in the market while Mickey pushed quarters into the machine and watched a canteen being magically filled with spring water. Then a shrill voice made him look up.

"I hate broccoli! Why can't we have hot dogs?"

A weary mother snapped, "All right, Billy! Hot dogs, just to keep you quiet. Stay here and watch our groceries."

Mickey switched canteens as the water continued to pour from the machine. Billy's attitude made him think the kid would benefit from being lost in the mountains and he couldn't help thinking 'there but for the grace of God go I.'

He realized then that the proverb was more complacent than thankful. It wasn't Billy's fault that he was spoiled. Something would make a man of him in time, unless he was being raised like a Chasen; then nothing would keep him from becoming an outlaw who despised humankind.

After a few minutes the bored hot dog lover pushed his grocery cart closer to ask Mickey, "Are you a drifter?"

"Mountaineer," Mickey decided to say.

"Is that real fur on your shoes?" the boy asked rudely.

"Rabbit fur." Mickey gestured to Sport, who was trailing the youngster. "There weren't any hot dogs where I was."

180

"I bet you're making that up. You're only trying to look like Mickey Barnes." Deeply angry about something, Billy kicked at the grocery cart.

"Pardon me?" Mickey hoped he had misunderstood.

The kid was scathing. "You can't be much of a mountaineer if you never heard of Mickey Barnes."

Mickey choked back a laugh. "The name's familiar."

"Man, don't you ever listen to the news?" Billy informed him with disgust, "Everybody knows how --"

"Billy, come here!" His mother scolded him, "I got your hot dogs and you've been told a hundred times not to talk to strangers!"

Sport had to leap out of Billy's way as he jerked the grocery cart around and jeered at Mickey, "He's the kid who drowned and lived in the mountains for a whole year so he could come back after everybody thought he was dead. He's got a dog that looks like that one over there and you don't even know who he is!"

Safe in his mother's grasp, he yelled at Mickey as she pulled him away, "I'll bet you sleep in your car!"

Mickey looked after the boy in mute astonishment. Shoppers were starting to stare at him and he picked up the water canteens to make his way quickly back to the car.

Locking the doors and sliding down behind the wheel to wait for Sport, he whispered, "What in the world is going on? When the truth hits that kid, he'll probably tell the cops to look for a teenage drifter sleeping in his car."

Sport ambled leisurely to the station wagon and Mickey drove around until it was time to pick up his suit. He felt like a giant spotlight was on them and he had to force himself to walk from the false security of the stolen station wagon into the dry cleaners, ten feet away. But the man only glanced at the clock on the wall and said proudly, "Here you go, son, an hour on the dot."

When Mickey hurried back to the station wagon a traffic cop was standing on the sidewalk to look it over. Sport was sitting tall in the driver's seat to look at the cop, and Mickey was steeled for the worst when the officer asked, "How do you like your new wagon?"

Mickey said, "It's not mine, actually. A guy asked me to drive it to his uncle's house so he could take the plane."

"How does your friend like it?" the officer inquired.

"What's not to like?" Mickey laughed. "It rides smooth as glass and has room to carry a ton of stuff." He decided not to say that he had planned to sleep in it during the trip.

The friendly cop confided, "That's why I want one, but paying interest on that much of a loan puts me off."

"I know what you mean." Mickey resisted the temptation to tell him that the car could be picked up for a song at Seventh and Wheeler in Kansas City. "I'll be lucky to be able to buy a motorbike."

"Is that your dog?" The cop smiled at the way Sport was peering in the rearview mirror as if he were driving.

Mickey said, "No, I'm taking him home so he won't have to be tranquilized out of his mind to fly."

"Very good," the cop approved. "Enjoy your trip."

"We will, thanks."

As Mickey headed out of town he told Sport, "That cop either figures it's none of his business how we get home or he missed the newscast Billy heard. I'd better back up our story by putting a memo in the glove compartment."

He changed his clothes in a gas station restroom and asked for some paper so he could write a note. All the attendant had was a standard service form, so Mickey wrote on the back, '*Leave the station wagon at 7th and Wheeler in KC by five p.m. Friday afternoon. Remind cousin Joe that the registration isn't in the car and say hello from his drinking buddies in Fort Collins. Thanks for the use of the wheels. MKB*'

When it began to get dark Mickey looked for a cheap motel that was off the highway. Seeing a sign for a Greyhound Bus Station, he knew that he would find a cafe and a decent motel nearby.

He parked behind a darkened post office and told Sport to wait in the car while he went to the motel across the street to get a room. He signed the register Gerry Harkness and when he was asked to add his license number he said, "I came in on the Greyhound. Do people still take cash?"

He put a fifty-dollar bill on the countertop and the grinning manager handed him a key as he said, "You bet. For twenty-five bucks you can have a single with TV but no phone. I don't suppose you brought any pets on the bus."

Mickey agreed, "That would have been awkward."

He dropped his backpack off in the room before hurrying back to tell Sport, "We're in, but don't walk too close."

The clever dog nosed at everything along the way as if he were alone. He lifted his leg on a water hydrant and lingered there until Mickey unlocked the door. Then he streaked into the motel room as if a bobcat were in pursuit.

Mickey bolted the door before he turned on the lights. After choosing their escape route, a bathroom window big enough to climb through, he took his first hot shower in a year. He was tempted to stay in until the hot water was gone but Sport was nervous about being trapped in the small furnished room. He had only been allowed in the screen-porch at home during thunderstorms, and Solomon's roomy cave had seemed like living outdoors.

When Mickey emerged from the steamy bathroom the wary Golden Retriever was prowling around the motel room sniffing at everything and making faces.

Mickey sympathized as he opened the windows, "It's not as clean as the mountains." One of the screens was missing, but he knew it wouldn't bother them if something flew in. He told Sport, "Lay low here and I'll be back as

183

soon as I've ordered a couple of doggie bags to go. I'll lock the room, but you're not trapped."

He paid for the food and told the woman at the cafe that he would come back in ten minutes to pick it up. Then he jogged back to the motel and was momentarily dismayed to find the room empty. Hoping the Retriever hadn't found it necessary to escape, he wet his lips to whisper, "Sport?"

The dog's black nose poked through a narrow crack in the bathroom door to admit that he was in hiding.

Mickey laughed with relief and told him, "Supper in ten minutes -- rare steak and grilled fish. Don't freak out when you see television for the first time in your life."

Sport sniffed at the talking face on the news just long enough to decide that it was an illusion. A minute later he stiffened to reflect Mickey's tension as the newscaster said,

"Tonight a mystery ended in Miracle Falls, Wyoming, only to create a more exciting mystery. The question uppermost in the minds of many Americans on this night is 'Where is Mickey Barnes?'"

Mickey gasped, "Oh god, I was afraid of that!" and Sport put his nose between his paws and whimpered.

"If you're wondering who Mickey Barnes is, chances are you're not from his home state of Kansas or living in Wyoming where five missing persons are the focus of daily conversation. To recap: Fourteen-year-old Mickey fell into the Metedeconk River last June and vanished without a trace. The family dog jumped in after him and likewise disappeared. Both were presumed drowned, but like others who vanished from the Pinecrest area, neither body was ever recovered.

"Last November a dazed youth claiming to be Mickey wandered into the town of Miracle Falls. He was not, to the tragic disappointment of Mickey's family and growing number of friends. Then last Wednesday a youth described by witnesses as a 'tough-fisted kid traveling with a mean-

184

looking dog' introduced himself to Miracle Falls' sheriff as Michael Karst Barnes.

"When a doubtful Sheriff Burnside offered to ship the teenager and his dog to Kansas City he found himself talking to thin air. Burnside chalked up yet another missing person, this time a nameless one.

"Now there's reason to believe that this new Mickey Barnes could be the real McCoy. A registered letter that documents several significant facts matches handwriting that was submitted by Mickey's brother for the purpose of comparison. It's the proof people have been waiting for.

"This self-sufficient young man wrote to the sheriff to explain his refusal to be flown home and he has communicated with the Barnes' family physician and minister. They are in agreement that he is Charles and Glenda Barnes missing son. So the only remaining question appears to be where is Mickey tonight?"

Mickey said, "Throwing up," and held his hand to his queasy stomach.

"Here's a news update that just came in. This afternoon professional spelunkers recovered human remains from a cave a few miles from the now-deserted Pinecrest Camp. The name 'Harold Simpson' and the date October Ninth, Nineteen thirty-two were written in blood on the wall of the cave a few feet from Simpson's remains.

"Even more interesting -- also printed in blood with the more recent date, June 27th, Nineteen seventy-nine -- is the name Michael K. Barnes. The fact that there are no remains with that incredible marker leaves little doubt that young Mickey shared that uncomfortable grave long enough to believe that it would be his final resting-place."

A MacDonald's commercial came on to remind Mickey that it was almost time to pick up their food. He switched to a different channel in time to hear an anchorwoman say, *"Experiments are underway to use bright-colored dyes to*

185

determine where that strong undertow takes its victims. An ancient Indian legend tells of an underground river that flows from the twisting Metedeconk to spectacular Miracle Falls. It appears at this moment in time that the myth could be a fact. One person who may have found the answer is the still missing Michael Barnes. Goodnight, Mickey, wherever you are."

Sport nudged at Mickey's tingling hand. He wanted his supper. Mickey's head was shaking back and forth to deny what he was hearing and Sport whined to nudge him again.

Mickey whispered, "First they don't believe us and now we're suddenly on the national news! How come? What made us that important?"

He wasn't prepared for fame! It would be easier to be labeled a teenage delinquent than the hero of a myth who had battled the wilderness single-handed and won.

He stammered, "They'll know I didn't do that alone. They'll see all those markers and find out that I was the one who shot Flag and Gary. Then they might find Solomon before he can turn himself in --"

Sport's teeth fastened on Mickey's jacket and he shook it from side to side.

Mickey argued, "Listen, we're in big trouble here, and all you can think of is your supper?"

Sport looked back at him without blinking an eye.

Mickey's breath escaped in a sigh and he slumped on the edge of the bed. "No, you want me to stop acting like a lunatic. You want me to get organized and start using my head instead of panicking."

He quoted Solomon to calm his fear. "'Know thyself; heal thyself.' We didn't count on national publicity, but we don't have to be swept along with it. It's not an undertow unless we let it be -- and it's not as if the Boy Scouts of America will expect me to give lectures on survival."

Realizing that they might expect just that, he said stubbornly, "What the heck, if civilization makes us feel like we're being held hostage we can go back to the mountains. All we have to do is go home long enough to show everyone that the trip didn't kill us."

Sport said he would go wherever Mickey went, but could he have his supper first?

Mickey apologized, "Of course, I'm sorry." Walking to the door, his appetite had flown and his watery legs reminded him of his weakness after the scorpion attack. He looked for something to be optimistic about and could only say, "It's a good thing they don't have a recent picture of us or I wouldn't be able to pick up our supper. All they've got is a fuzzy photo of a funny-looking little boy."

Chapter Twenty-four

The KC Carni-Co carried everything from party goods to collapsible carnival booths. Mickey's mother loved to tell how her nine-year-old had bought a roll of nickel tickets so he could sell 'magic woods tours' behind his house. Then he had used the profit to buy a roll of twenty-five cent tickets for a sidewalk comic book sale.

The store had been one of Mickey's favorite places to browse but he doubted that the owners would recognize him. The little man had found ringing up sales with his antique cash register more important than remembering customer's names. His wife, a tiny blonde with a reedy voice, had been filling an order the last time Mickey was in the store, nearly two years ago. But although twenty dollars had seemed like a lot to spend on decorations for Hodge's surprise party, Mickey's determination to get his money's worth hadn't impressed the proprietors of the Carni-Co.

Now he found out that the two were sharp when it came to doing business. When he explained what he wanted to achieve, the little man warned, "That won't be cheap, son. You're talkin' about two-three hours work plus all the stuff to fancy up your station wagon."

Mickey set a time limit. "Keep it to an hour and a half and only use as much as it takes to make the car parade

188

worthy. Seventy-five dollars?" Now that his cash was running low he was impersonating a college freshman on his way home for the summer.

The proprietor's wife piped, "Ninety-five."

Mickey gave her a hundred and said, "It doesn't have to be beautiful, just attract a lot of attention. I want every eye on that car, understand?" He picked up a ball for Sport and said, "I'll take this for my change."

"You got it, babe," the tiny woman trilled. "Good thing your car's light-colored; that'll set off our decorations." She winked at her husband and teased Mickey, "Goin' home in style, huh?"

He had to say, "It's not for me. I'm returning the car for a roommate who decided to take the train."

Her husband mentioned, "We thought you might be doing it for the big celebration out in Overland Park. This is Mickey Barnes Day, you know."

Mickey was startled and had to look away as he said, "I avoid crowds as a rule. Parades aren't my thing."

"Just your friend's thing, huh?" The proprietor rang up the sale in his antique cash register and promised, "We'll fix his car up good. That your yellow pooch by the door?"

Surprised to see Sport peering through the glass door, Mickey tried to laugh it off. "He seems to think so."

Sport had been asked to hang out at the barbershop and Mickey hurried out to whisper, "What's your problem?"

Sport admitted that he was suffering from impatience.

Mickey walked the Golden Retriever away from the Carni-Co as he said, "I know, me too. But Dr. Harkness and Reverend Hasty need time to lay the groundwork so the family won't freak out when they see us."

The morning news on the car radio had reported that phone calls to Mickey's home were being screened through an answering service. Glenda and Charlie Barnes weren't available for comment and Chuck had told the press that he would believe it when he saw it.

Dozens of crank calls had been made by teenagers pretending to be Mickey and people had reported seeing him in places where he couldn't possibly have been.

Jean and Billy had both been interviewed on television, and the elated salesclerk in Albuquerque had bragged about selling every suit in the store after telling the press how Mickey had fooled him. When the interviewer asked, "Where do you think Mickey got all that money?" the clerk had replied reverently, "He could have sold a couple of his handmade suits. I've never seen anything so beautiful."

Even the cop who had admired the station wagon had shared his story, adding that he hadn't found it necessary to report the incident so Mickey and Sport could be given a police escort to Overland Park. He said, "The kid seemed to know what he was doing and I couldn't see any reason why he shouldn't be allowed to do it his way."

Only Skinhead and the Beard hadn't taken a turn in the spotlight, and it was easy to guess why.

Mickey decided to try calling home from a pay phone. When he was asked for his name he said, "I just need you to tell Dr. Harkness that dot-to-dot Scar-hip will be home at six-thirty barring complications. He's in east Topeka now." A forgivable lie to throw the press off the track.

"Who is this?" the operator asked quickly.

Mickey replied "Allison's boyfriend's brother," and hung up to break the connection.

Since he couldn't drive around until it was time to go home it seemed like a good idea to hang out in a park. He figured that no one would expect a budding celebrity to kill an hour and a half by playing ball with his famous dog. But after they got to the park he realized that anyone with a Golden Retriever would be suspect on Mickey Barnes Day.

He and Sport needed to separate but stay in communicating distance in case of an emergency. It was easy for Mickey to blend into a crowd, but a dog that wasn't on a leash on the city streets was bound to attract attention.

Pretending to shop at a Woolworth's five and dime appeared to be a better plan, so Sport crouched behind a portable trash bin in the alley to wait for him.

As Mickey drifted from counter to counter, the unnerving sight of a surveillance camera made him decide to tell the girl at the cash register that he had forgotten his list and he needed to see if he could recreate it.

She said as she handed him a pencil and paper, "I've done that a dozen times, but I've never tried to rewrite it."

After spending several minutes listing practical items Mickey took his time finding them. Seeing a small camera and a shoulder strap case that would hold his purchases, he realized that when he got close to home he could pretend to be a rookie reporter assigned to cover Mickey Barnes Day.

He saw a condensed version of Roget's Thesaurus on a rotating bookrack near the checkout counter and remembered how Solomon had called the book necessary for survival in civilization. The bubbly cashier confided as he picked it up, "I love that little book! Are you a writer?"

Mickey said, "Not yet, but I plan to have a lot of things to write about during the next year."

It was fun thinking that she might report sighting him, but he knew that the press wouldn't be satisfied with talking to the people he met on his way home. He would need to give them a statement before long, and a pocket-sized edition of Solomon's favorite book would come in handy.

By the time he circled back through the alley to let Sport know that the longest hour and a half of their life had passed, he needed to calm his butterflies by getting a hamburger. He had realized that his stubborn desire to get himself and Sport home under their own power might have to

191

be sacrificed if they were cornered by reporters or police. The most important thing was to act with dignity, and not just for the sake of his family.

Now that he was being regarded as a returning hero it would be easy to explain the stolen car and lack of a driver's license, but having a police escort to Overland Park would be almost as unnerving as being flown to the juvenile authorities in Kansas City.

The decorated station wagon was parked in the delivery area behind the Carni-Co. Mickey had to laugh when he saw it. Purple, orange and lavender were mixed in a gaudy combination of rosettes and streamers that completely covered the car. The doors were canary-yellow and the windows were framed in shocking pink.

Mickey congratulated the decorators, "That's perfect!"

The little woman told him, "You said it didn't have to be beautiful, but this is how Earnie and me started out in the business and once we got started we couldn't stop."

Her husband assured Mickey with a shy smile, "There's no charge for all the extra stuff because we took pictures to show our customers. Hope ya' don't mind."

"Not at all. It looks sensational." Mickey held the door open for Sport and said, "Hop in, son, let's go."

Sport sniffed at the decorations. His nose wrinkled with distaste and he backed off to bark at the car.

"Don't start that." Mickey argued, "Just for five blocks. Three minutes, tops. It won't hurt, honest."

Sport sat down to say that he would prefer to walk.

"Dammit, we're in this thing together." Mickey scolded the suspicious dog, "Listen, if you'd had any objection to this car you should have said so back in Fort Collins where it would have done some good."

Sport glared at him. That wasn't fair. The car looked different then and it didn't smell so bad.

192

The man took a picture of them as Mickey bargained, "You can sit on the floor where nobody will see you. Cripes, no one's going to blame a dog for decorating a car! Do you want to go home with me or don't you?"

Sport trudged slowly to the car, jumped in and hunched down with his chin resting on the passenger seat.

The little woman clapped her hands with delight and told her husband, "I told you we used too much purple, Earnie. Get one more picture of them driving away."

Mickey waved and called, "Thanks again." He was glad they were taking pictures because he had neglected to buy any film for his camera.

Drivers honked at the sight of the decorated station wagon as Mickey drove into the street and he prayed, "God, don't let us get stuck in traffic. Four more blocks... I should have checked out that intersection! Maybe there's no parking lot. It could be high-rise buildings by now. I swear, after we unload this car I'm not driving again until I get a license! Seventh street; there it is, thank you, God."

He parked the station wagon facing Wheeler Street where all of Kansas City could view the bizarre apparition. Any thief would hesitate to pick up that stolen car, but a true Cousin Joe would laugh his head off and drive it until the last rosette fell off.

Leaving the car keys under the passenger seat, Mickey knew that Flag would have enjoyed his joke on a small-time crook. He walked away carrying his backpack and camera case and Sport scooted to the corner where he could use the crosswalk and stay in sight across the street.

As Mickey headed for a hotel where taxicabs were waiting for fares he was stopped cold by a huge banner on a coffee shop that shouted WELCOME HOME, MICKEY!

A few people were glancing at Sport as he wove his way through the pedestrian traffic but nobody was giving Mickey a second look. The grease-burger he had eaten too fast had turned to a rock in his tight stomach and he was reminded of Solomon's warning. *'You might find the city a more dangerous wilderness than an innocent forest, and you'll need to stay in readiness to defend yourself.'*

Sport decided to sit in the shade of the hotel awning to wait for his partner to catch up. Mickey crossed the street at the next corner and walked to the nearest cab to ask the driver, "Taxi?"

The driver scowled and said, "I don't take animals."

Mickey looked at the dog standing beside him and couldn't deny that they were together. A couple of women who had emerged from the hotel were looking at them and whispering. For an anxious moment Mickey wished he had driven the station wagon all the way home instead of leaving it at the drop-off point. As Sport waited for him to decide what to do, a stout redheaded woman ground out her cigarette and offered, "I take dogs, monkeys, drunks..." She opened her cab door to tell Mickey, "Pile in, honey. This is the wrong day to refuse a dog."

He tossed his pack in the cab and said, "Thanks!"

Sport looked the redhead and her taxi over more carefully before deciding that it would be okay if Mickey opened the window to let in some fresh air.

The redheaded cabby razzed them as she pushed down the meter, "Who belongs to who?"

Mickey said, "I used to be his, but we're equals now." Hoping that this would be the final leg of their journey, he told her, "We're going to Marty Street in Overland Park."

"You joke." She informed him, "The traffic is murder from State Line Road, but I'll get you as close as I can." She threw her cab in gear and slipped into traffic as if she were driving a Mack truck before telling him, "Mickey's coming home this afternoon. Don't you know that?"

So much for best-laid plans. They would have to separate and circle through the woods. The crowd would spot

194

Chuck's Retriever before they would recognize Mickey by his pug-nosed smile, and Sport was becoming an expert at creating a diversion.

Mickey decided, "You can stop before you get stuck in traffic and we'll walk in. We're very good at walking."

"Oh my god..." The cab driver's face paled and her eyes filled with tears as she moaned, "Lord save us!"

Afraid she might be having a stroke Mickey asked, "What's wrong?"

Her hand clutched at her throat and her foot hit the brake to stop for a yellow light as she choked, "Are you --" She panted helplessly before she could say, "him?"

Mickey didn't know whether to throw himself on her mercy or get out of the taxi and take his chances on foot. The fact that Sport had decided the redhead was okay encouraged him to say, "Take it easy, I'm really a very normal person."

He was ready to run like hell, was that normal? "Sport's a lot friendlier than he looks. It's just that his head got kind of creased."

Sport cleared his throat and his warm brown eyes smiled at the emotional female who was frozen at the wheel staring at them in the rearview mirror. Mascara streamed down her cheeks and she looked like a circus clown weeping, "God love ya', child, is it really you?"

"I'm afraid so." Touched and embarrassed, Mickey was afraid that things were going to get wetter out before the storm blew over. He explained earnestly, "The trouble is, we never pictured all of this. We figured it would only be the family and us. My dad had a stroke, and my mom may not recognize me."

The redhead was nodding and gulping back tears that ran down her rouged cheeks. "Oh, you poor, sweet baby."

"It's not that bad, honest." Mickey's laugh shook and he insisted, "We're both fine." He warned the Retriever whose eyes were suspiciously bright, "Don't you start crying or we'll all drown. Listen, Miss --"

"It's Maida," she reached for a tissue to blow her nose. "I'm Maida, and I'll be all right. It's just that you gave me such a turn, appearing out of nowhere like that."

Mickey realized it might never be more important for him to stay in control and he said calmly, "I think it's really nice that people want to celebrate with us, but --"

"I know, I know," Maida mopped at her tears. "You need time alone with your family. Your dear mother needs that, God love her."

"Exactly." Mickey found Maida's outburst unsettling but he knew they were in the right cab. "If we can keep from adding to the madness, we'll find a way to do that."

"You betcha!" She hunched over the wheel, ready to take orders and vowed, "I'm with you all the way. I'll drive through fire."

"I don't think that will be necessary." Humbled by her devotion on such short acquaintance Mickey cautioned, "Just don't do anything to attract attention."

Sport's eyes were laughing at him and Mickey said, "Don't rub it in, okay?"

Now he knew why the owners of the Carni-Co had taken all those pictures. A million newspapers would probably carry a front-page photo of him coaxing Sport to get into the decorated station wagon. That would give Skinhead and the Beard a turn, to say the least.

Chapter Twenty-five

Overland Park was normally a quiet suburb where there were almost as many rabbits and squirrels as people, but now the traffic was backed-up six miles from Mickey's house. Cars were parked bumper-to-bumper on every side street as well as on vacant lots, and even on lawns where residents were charging parking fees.

People were walking in carrying folding chairs and baskets of food, the way they would for a picnic at the park. The mood was festive and no one seemed a stranger to anyone else. They were all strangers to Mickey, or people who had changed as much he had in less than a year.

Maida joked, "It looks like they're expecting you to show up in your mountaineering clothes with Sportin' Life toting a backpack that's labeled 'Here's Mickey!'"

Mickey laughed, glad that she had recovered from her initial shock. Then he warned, "Here comes a traffic cop."

Sport crouched on the car floor as the officer approached to tell Maida, "Through traffic only."

She nodded and agreed, "Goin' through, officer."

The cop blew his whistle to start the cross traffic moving and she muttered, "I'm goin' through all right. Only you n' Sport are gettin' off."

Sport's nose was raised, smelling things that reminded him of home, and Mickey detected new smells that were almost as puzzling to him as they were to the sensitive dog. Looking around at familiar terrain, he made an easy decision. "I'm going over the side of that hill."

"Are you sure?" Maida questioned the wisdom of his plan. "That's a pretty steep climb."

Mickey laughed at her motherly concern. "It's a very small hill, Maida, and besides, my house is over there through a bunch of trees."

He had called that bunch of trees 'the woods' until he lived in a forest, and he added uncertainly, "Unless the land was subdivided while I was gone and houses were built."

He hoped with all his heart that his miniature woods still existed, and not just because of his need today.

"No tract, Mickey," Maida assured him. "A group of overnight campers got chased out of there early this morning and the police assigned guards to keep people out."

Mickey said confidently, "I'll get through. Drop me off at the base of the hill and take Sport to the movie theater in the middle of town. He knows his way home from there. When you let him out, yell 'Go Sport' as loud as you can."

Sport stiffened at the command and Mickey told him, "Not yet, partner, in a little while. Then head home like a shot to create a diversion." He bragged to Maida, "This is a move we've had to master, living in the wilderness and returning to civilization. It may be why we're still intact."

Maida said, "I'll take your word for it, honey. You sure know a lot of fancy words."

Mickey told her, "That may keep us intact. I need to ask for a favor. I can only carry what a reporter would have so I'll have to leave my backpack --"

"You'll have it the minute you call me," Maida promised. "Are you about ready to make your move?"

198

"Yes." Mickey told the eager Golden Retriever, "You need to go with Maida. I'll meet you at home, understand?"

Sport understood. He was more excited than nervous, and Mickey told Maida, "Now." She stopped just long enough for him to slide out and he said, "Okay, go!"

Heading for the hill at a run, he was feeling more optimistic than he had when he left home eleven months ago. A traffic cop whistled shrilly at him, but by the time he could call in his report Mickey was on his way up the hill.

The ground was uneven, with no path to show that anyone ever came this way. There were boulders and thick bushes and Mickey had to remind himself that he didn't need to reach the top of the hill until Sport was starting to race home from the theater.

He was prepared to see people sitting on the hillside to look down at his house on its acre of woods, but the size of the gathering took his breath away. His wildest dreams of a welcome home hadn't even come close to this scene, and now he was worried about leaving Sport on his own.

Badly off-balance for a moment, he dealt with his fear by putting his plan into action. Establishing the role he had chosen, he made his way down the hill pretending to shoot pictures of the crowd.

He could see two or three news photographers and he imitated their actions. Halfway down the slope he stopped to ask some children who were selling a litter of mixed-breed puppies, "Any sign of him yet?"

According to his calculations Sport was halfway home, flying like the wind, and he took a minute to steady his heartbeat as the oldest boy replied, "Not yet, but we've got the best spot to see Mickey first."

He pretended to take their picture as he said, "You sure have. Your pups look thirsty; do you have any water?"

The boy said, "Only soda pop, and they don't like it."

199

A woman who was sitting a few feet away offered, "I brought a gallon of water and I'll be happy to share some."

Mickey said, "Thanks," knowing that the sooner he got himself home the better off everyone would be. He couldn't help saying before he moved on, "It might be a good idea not to handle your pups too much."

Making his way down the hill between groups of people who were playing cards or slathering on suntan lotion, he could hear them exchanging exaggerated tales about Mickey Barnes. The ground was being littered with fast food trash and he could imagine Solomon's reaction to hearing about this adventure.

Four uniformed officers had been assigned to guard the edge of the woods and Mickey approached the nearest one to say, "I need to get a shot of the hill through the trees."

The cop laughed and said, "Nice try." His duty was to control an excited crowd and keep pushy reporters in their place. "Nobody goes through these trees today."

Mickey zipped his camera in the case as he joked, "How about MKB? Is he allowed in?"

The cop told him, "Our hero is going to make a grand entrance in a decorated Chrysler station wagon, which won't come as a surprise to anyone who knows Mickey."

Sport would be getting close to home by now and Mickey wet his lips to ask, "Where did you hear that?"

The cop took pleasure in telling a rookie, "He was spotted at the Carni-Co getting the car decorated. The owners reported that the dog was a dead-ringer for Sport and Mickey was devouring a double-whopper like he hadn't tasted one for a year."

Mickey said, "Proof positive." Then he winced as the roaring crowd rose like bats flying out of a cave, cheering as if the home team had just scored a winning touchdown.

The grinning cop yelled over the noise, "That's it, Mickey's home!"

People were shouting, "There's Sport! Look at that crazy dog run! There's Chuck, but where's Mickey?"

"Hey!" The cop yelled as Mickey took off through the woods, "Come back here!"

Mickey didn't slow down as he shouted, "I can't come back, I live here!"

It figured that more policemen would be stationed in the woods and he sidestepped a flying tackle. The agile cop managed to snag the strap of the camera case and Mickey let him have it, needing only his legs to get him home.

As he emerged from the trees at the edge of his backyard he wasn't surprised to be grabbed and held tightly by two officers who snapped, "No reporters!"

Sport was racing in circles around the backyard with Chuck in joyous pursuit. Skidding into Mickey, he barked sharply at the officers, giving them clear orders to back off!

Mickey could hear the excited crowd starting to close in as Chuck dashed up to glare at him and tell the cops, "I can't believe these people!"

Mickey ordered, "Chuck, tell them who I am!"

One of the officers asked, "Do you know this guy?" and Chuck went into a slow freeze.

The security of home seemed a mile away and the back door of the house was about to be blocked by howling humanity. Chuck was staring at Mickey's dark, windblown hair and grown-up body and Mickey's voice cracked as he growled, "Dammit, Chuck, I'm your brother!"

Sport tore off to stand halfway between them and the back door. He barked without stopping, telling Mickey to hurry and warning others to stay away.

Mickey grabbed his brother's limp hand to plead, "Wake up, will you? Don't do this to me!"

The cop demanded, "Do you know him or don't you?"

Mickey chattered desperately, "I'll give up listening to my comics on the day you stop reading your stupid rock and roll music!"

Chuck's lips pressed lips together and he panted helplessly before he could say, "He's my brother. It's Mickey."

"Okay! Now move it!" Mickey ran for the door, dragging Chuck after him. Suddenly afraid that the door might be locked, he could see himself trapped halfway inside, crushed to death by fans celebrating his triumphant return.

To his vast relief the door banged open, and he gasped, "Go, Sport!"

Sport started inside and stopped, remembering that his place was outside, not in Mrs. Barnes' dogless house.

A thousand voices were yelling, *Mickey!*" and he gave Sport's rump a blunt kick from behind to pull Chuck in after him and bolt the door.

It was over at last; they were home.

Chapter Twenty-six

"We made it!" Mickey leaned against the door and mopped at his forehead with his sleeve. "My god, this is worse than being lost in the mountains."

He apologized to Sport for the kick and knew that he was forgiven. His dad's green cardigan was lying on a towel on top of the washing machine, and seeing the red and white-checkered curtains in the kitchen made Mickey feel like his best dream had come true.

Chuck looked like he was still trying to find his little brother in a lanky stranger and Mickey advised, "Relax for a minute and catch your breath. There's no hurry now. Sorry I had to pressure you out there, but I was afraid we were about to be crushed by the mob."

The clamor was starting to subside and he could hear the cops asking people to move away from the house to give the family some privacy.

Chuck nodded and a sigh escaped his loose lips. He looked haggard, definitely on the sleepless side, but Mickey would have known him anywhere. It could have been five minutes since Chuck had said that the fishing would be better on the other side of the lake.

"You do know me..." Mickey discovered that his older brother was shorter than he was. Chuck had gotten heavier and his conservative haircut made him look like a traveling salesman. Mickey smiled and said, "Hello?" Voices deepened, but smiles hardly ever changed.

Chuck's voice shook saying, "I know you... Oh god, Mickey." His swimming eyes looked down at Sport and he said, "It's just --" Words failed him and he shook his head.

Sport looked from Chuck's face to Mickey's and he whined, wondering why they had stopped here. Then he sat down to wait for them to finish whatever they were doing.

Mickey gave Chuck a tight hug and wanted to say that tears weren't a sign of weakness, only of sensitivity. He stepped back to say instead, "Hey, only a frog could stay dry-eyed at a time like this."

"Right." A helpless laugh shook Chuck and he apologized, "The thing is, I was afraid to let myself believe it, even after I saw Sport. You're so much ..."

Mickey said, "Older. A lot older. How's Dad?"

"Sedated." Chuck had to clear his throat before he could say, "Try not to look shocked when you see him. Dad's changed as much as you have and he's worried about how he'll look to you, among other things..."

Mickey promised, "I'll watch that. What other things?" Sport was trying to figure out how to get himself to the screen porch without having to walk through the house.

"Well," Chuck's mouth twisted. "We made you go fishing that day --"

Mickey stopped him. "I'm not buying guilt from anyone. The truth is I'm better off for the trip. Is Mom okay?"

"The 'trip?'" Chuck uttered a disbelieving laugh. He dried his cheeks with his hands and took a breath to get a fresh grip on himself. "Mom's fine. Mostly she takes care of Dad. That's the way it is now. Dad's her baby." He looked down at the permanent crease on Sport's head and sighed. "You guys look like you've been through a war."

The crowd was starting to sing a peace song Mickey had never heard before and he said, "The war's over."

"Right." Chuck's smile wobbled and he mentioned, "Incidentally, a few people are here."

Mickey had to laugh. "We noticed that."

"I mean in the house. Maybe Sport had better stay --"

"No, we're in this together." Mickey wasn't going any place where his partner wasn't welcome, especially at home, and Sport pressed against his leg to agree that neither of them would face any challenge alone.

Chuck nodded. "Okay, I'm with you. Let's go."

He murmured as they walked through the kitchen, "Everyone was expecting you to arrive in a station wagon decorated to the bumpers. Don't ask why."

Mickey said, "We know why."

Sport was hanging back, afraid of being scolded for entering the house, and Mickey stopped at the door to the dining room. The place looked like a tornado had touched down to leave punch glasses and finger sandwiches scattered in its path, and there were at least twenty-five people crowded into the tiny living room.

Looking for a familiar face, Mickey's hope of a quiet family reunion flew out the window. He saw Reverend Hasty talking to a distinguished-looking gentleman who could be a TV newscaster. Dr. Harkness was peering out the front window, no doubt looking for Mickey, and Danny Carlin was standing in the corner with a beautiful brunette who was probably Allison. All the rest were strangers.

Mickey found his mother easily although she was thinner and her hair had been styled at the beauty parlor. She looked stiff, ready to shatter, and her trim navy blue dress looked like someone else had chosen it for the occasion.

A surge of sympathy made Mickey want to protect her from all the unwanted attention and he felt like telling

Chuck to ask the party guests if they would mind waiting outside with the people gathered in front of the house.

Dr. Harkness said, "I don't see Sport or Mickey, but the crowd must have seen both of them because they've quieted down and they're singing."

Chuck stepped into the dining room to say, "Mom?"

Sport was by his side and she put her hand to her throat to gasp, "Oh, Sport! It's really you, after all this time."

She looked beyond the tall stranger who stood in the doorway, trying to find her son. Then her eyes shot back to him and she whispered in disbelief, "*Mickey?*"

He nodded, unable to speak, and she ran to him crying, "Oh, son! Oh Mickey, you're home!"

More helpless in her embrace than he had felt since he woke up in the cave, it was all he could do to say, "It's me, Mom." He hadn't realized until now how small his mother was, and he managed to whisper, "I'm sorry I couldn't keep your little boy from growing up."

"Oh, darling... my darling son!"

She was laughing through her tears and Mickey could feel her thoughts the same way he sensed Sport's feelings. But he was unable to interpret them because his mother's mind seemed to run in circles.

She released him to say, "Let me look at you. Merciful heavens, you're a grown man!" Pulling him toward an old man in a wheelchair, she sounded like she was speaking to a child as she said, "Charlie, look here. This is your son, Mickey! Isn't he the living image of my brother Jack?"

Chuck's hand on Mickey's shoulder reminded him not to reveal his shock and Sport pressed closer as he made himself smile and say, "It's probably the hair."

His dad was old, actually *infirmed*. As fast as Mickey's mind found the word he erased it, but he knew that nothing could have prepared him for the heartbreaking sight of the

206

graying man who sat slumped off-balance with the left side of his body hanging slack.

Mickey felt nine years old saying, "I need a haircut."

Joyous laughter relieved the tension in the room. Compared to Chuck, Mickey looked like a homeless hermit, and he tried to pretend that no one else was in the room as he knelt beside the wheelchair to take his father's hand.

Charlie's dark eyes were fearful and Mickey's voice was huskier than usual trying to comfort him. "I was waiting until I got home so you could cut my hair."

It was no use; he had changed too much for his dad to know him. Charlie pushed slurring words through drooping lips. "Not much va' barber n'more. Had a s'roke and s'all I can do t'talk. Zat the watch I gave you? It looks broke."

He squinted at it suspiciously and Mickey said, "It's the same one, Dad. I had to make a new watchband and it needs a battery." He wished he had remembered to do that when he was killing time at Woolworth's.

Charlie leaned forward in his wheelchair to peer uncertainly at Mickey. After a long moment he said doubtfully, "You look real good, son," and then he jerked away to ask, "Glenda, is this one Mickey?"

She said firmly, "Yes, Charlie, he really is."

Chuck backed her up. "He just got a little older. A lot older, actually."

Mickey told his father, "You're not dreaming and neither am I. This time it's real and we're going to be all right." He looked at his mother to vow, "That's a promise."

Suddenly filled with unreasonable guilt, he wondered if it was because of being dumb enough to fall overboard. He told himself that the guests who witnessed his vow had every right to be there. His dad was afraid to face him, so friends who had helped his family through an impossible year had come to lessen the anxiety and verify the miracle.

207

Sheriff Burnside was hiding behind Reverend Hasty and Mickey had a new appreciation of the sheriff's grim determination to protect the Barnes family from any more pain. Their war had been worse than his and Sport's.

Dr. Harkness came to shake Mickey's hand and say, "Welcome home, son." He gave him a bear hug to murmur, "You look absolutely splendid."

Mickey was surrounded with congratulations and Sport stayed close by his side to remind him that they could go back to the mountains if they didn't like it here.

Kansas City's mayor gave Mickey a stack of telegrams that included messages from the governors of Colorado, Kansas and Wyoming. Danny Carlin gripped Mickey's hand to say, "I'm really glad you won't have to sick your vicious dog on me."

Allison's dark-lashed blue eyes sparkled with tears and her voice was velvet-soft saying, "Hello, Michael, we've all been praying for you."

Mickey said, "That may be why I'm here." He could see why anyone would fall in love with Allison, and a glance at Chuck made him decide that he would be wise to keep a safe distance between himself and his brother's girl.

As Reverend Hasty introduced him to people who seemed to know him better than he knew himself, it occurred to Mickey that his unbelievable homecoming was as transitory as being lost in the cave or imprisoned by the Chasens. Life was a snow shelter, after all.

The editor of a Kansas City newspaper said, "We'll get out of your way in a minute, Mick, but I need to ask a few questions -- like what happened to your classy wheels?"

Glad for the opportunity to explain that, Mickey said, "I decorated the car because I thought it might be stolen. A couple of guys at the campus in Fort Collins let me take it without asking to see a driver's license, and when I saw that there was no registration in the glove compartment I wanted them to get whatever they had coming."

Everyone laughed like he had pulled the greatest practical joke of all time and Allison said, "I'll drink to that."

She brought him a glass of punch and Sport barked happily, wanting to share it. Mickey told him, "You don't like fruit juice. I'll get you some water."

Chuck offered, "I'll take care of that. Come on, Sport."

Sport looked up at Mickey and sat down to wait for his water. Mickey was embarrassed for Chuck and he joked, "He'd like it in a bowl with no ice and he'll settle for whatever you've got on tap if there's no spring water."

Chuck said, "Oy, vot have you done to my dog?" but Mickey hoped that their sibling rivalry wouldn't be complicated by jealousy when the glow of his return faded.

He glanced at his mother to see if she shared his concern but she was steadying his dad's hand to keep a glass of punch from spilling on his white shirt. Recording that sad picture, he realized that their innocent image of Mickey and the pug-nosed smile had probably frozen in time.

Sheriff Burnside started to mumble an apology and Mickey shook his hand to say warmly, "Thanks for coming. If I can help with any of your mysteries, let me know."

He hoped that the sheriff would come to his senses by the time the truth began to surface, but the only thing he could be certain of was that they would meet again under equally trying circumstances.

The sheriff said humbly, "Thanks, I'd appreciate that."

The dark-suited gentleman who looked like a newscaster turned out to be a New York publisher. Mickey started to say that writing a book was the furthest thing from his mind and he remembered telling the talkative clerk at Woolworth's that he planned to have a lot to write about during the coming year.

He felt like a dolt when Reverend Hasty explained, "Mr. Fields lost his daughter at Pinecrest seven years ago. He promised your family that the search wouldn't be called off until some kind of tangible evidence was found."

Mickey lowered his voice to say, "Let's talk later. I have something to tell you and this is the wrong place."

Mr. Fields agreed, "Whenever you say." He walked to the dining room table to stand staring at the refreshments for a moment before he filled his glass to drink thirstily.

The editor who had been following Mickey around asked him, "So tell me; how does it feel to be home?"

Mickey found his question incredibly dumb, but the room quieted and everyone was waiting to hear his answer.

He decided to say politely, "Would you excuse me for a minute? I need to say hello to a few people outside so they can go home."

Danny whispered, "Good shot!" and Allison lifted her glass as Chuck said, "I'll drink to that."

Sport trotted to the door and Mickey's mother worried, "Oh, darling, do you think you should? Those people have come from all over, and there's a lot of flu going around."

Charlie roused to say gruffly, "Let 'im go, Mother. The boy can take care of himself."

Mickey said, "That's right, Dad. With Chuck on one side and Sport on the other, we're invulnerable to attack." He felt able to conduct a mob like an orchestra, and as he set down his empty glass he realized that the innocent tasting fruit drink packed a punch like a wine apple.

Chapter Twenty-seven

As Mickey stepped through the door onto his brightly lit front porch a welcoming shout rose from the huge crowd that stretched all the way from his trampled front yard to the curve in the street, nearly a block away.

People were sitting on the tops of cars and in trees to catch a glimpse of a returning hero and Mickey felt like a miscast character in a comic book. He and Hodge had fantasized about becoming famous for performing heroic deeds, but he was even less prepared to play an honest-to-god hero than he had been to survive in the wilderness.

Spotlights beamed from the backs of three remote television trucks blinded him, and his reaction to the crowd's emotion was interfering with Solomon's teaching about the confident use of language and the power of directed emotion. A dozen reporters were calling questions and Mickey knew that millions of people would hear his answers.

He had prepared a press statement to avoid answering questions when he and Sport were driving down dark roads for home. Now his mind was blank except for the warning: *'Display fear, be awkward in response, and men will use you to their personal gain.'*

The cheering went on and on and his smile was beginning to feel like a tire track carved in the mud. Sport sat

211

down to wait for him to make up his mind and Chuck stepped back as a reporter shouted over the noise, "Mickey, how does it feel to be home?"

Mickey said, "Would you excuse me for a minute? There are some people I need to see."

Sport started down the steps, then he stopped to ask if he could wait on the porch. Mickey realized that he would be walled in by strangers who would want to touch him and maybe clip off a souvenir wisp of hair. Sport didn't trust himself to accept that kind of love, and Mickey said, "Sure, wait here. Chuck can come with me."

Chuck squared his shoulders to agree, "You bet."

Police guards flanked them as they walked down the front steps together. Now words came easily. Mickey could say, "Thanks for coming," and let people pump his hands up and down or kiss them tearfully.

Old ladies pulled him into their arms to say, "We're so glad you're home safe," and Mickey repeated, "Thanks, I'm grateful to be back."

The police officer he had tangled with in the woods tossed him his camera case by the broken strap and razzed, "I hope there was some film in your camera."

Mickey laughed and admitted, "I wish there had been."

He heard a familiar Indian whoop and saw a hand waving wildly from several feet away. He called, "Hodge!" and made his way through more strangers to find a group of friends from school. He looked down at chunky, fat-cheeked Hodge and barely had time to say, "Welcome to chaos castle," before Lillian Merch grabbed him to give him a moist kiss on the mouth.

She looked like a cover girl for *Seventeen* and Mickey hoped no one was taking his picture with lipstick smeared on his mouth as he said, "My, how you've grown."

She pushed an autograph book at him and shrieked, "Oh, Mickey, you're unbelievable!"

He scribbled *'So are you, MKB'* and he still couldn't see why Hodge had been madly in love with Lillian.

A shy girl whose name he couldn't recall loaned him a handkerchief to wipe off the lipstick and Chuck teased him, "You'll need a personal manager if this keeps up."

Shifted from one group to the next, Mickey felt like he had jumped into a swift-moving stream. When a red-faced man challenged him, "Betcha don't remember me, Mick," all he could think of was dill pickles and he made a guess; "The delicatessen?" The thrilled owner of the deli grabbed his hand to squeeze it and say, "That's right!"

An elderly neighbor pleaded, "Try to stay your natural self, honey. Don't let all of this go to your head."

Mickey laughed. "Don't worry, Mrs. Thornbury, it probably won't last that long."

Mr. Thornbury said wryly, "Don't count on it, Mick. Real live heroes are getting damn hard to find."

Mickey's smile faded and he promised, "I'll watch it." He wished people could take shots for fame like the flu.

He looked for Ruby Ashton and understood why she would prefer to wait for a private visit. Ruby had hired teenagers to weed her garden after she reached the age of ninety, telling them that junk food would kill them as fast as cigarettes. Mickey hoped she still grew vegetables and herbs because he would need them to neutralize his mother's abundant servings of meat, pasta and desserts.

He told himself that it would be crazy to try and talk to everyone. Sport was starting to worry and the cops had put in a long day. He circled back to the porch, responding to strangers and finding a few more people he knew. He thought about asking Chuck to act as his manager until the madness wore off. Solomon had told him that asking for a favor could strengthen a friendship as long as the favor wasn't treated like a debt.

213

When he got back to the porch the journalists shoved microphones at him and he smiled to tell them, "Just don't ask me how it feels to be home."

A man's voice called over the laughter and applause, "You already told us!" and Mickey pointed at him to say, "That's right, in one word. Good."

He took the microphone from the nearest reporter's hand to ask, "Could I borrow this for a minute?"

"Sure." The surprised reporter laughed with the crowd.

'Know when to be still, and you'll be able to face any situation with a smile. You will serve no god but your own.'

Mickey closed his eyes to wait until the crowd was quiet and it became as still as the inside of a cave. When he began to speak, the depth in his amplified voice surprised him, echoing into the starry night.

"I dreamed about coming home a hundred times when I was lying in quiet places, thinking about this place and these people, but I never pictured a welcome like this...

"I will never forget this night. I want to thank Danny Carlin for his trust, and Dr. Harkness and Reverend Hasty for all they've done to make things easier for my family. I want to express my appreciation to Sheriff Burnside for caring enough about my family to make me prove who I was. He made me realize how much we've all changed.

"There's a publisher inside from New York -- his name slips my mind, but he's been a port in a storm, comforting my family and conducting an ongoing search.

"A cab driver offered to drive through fire so we could come home the way we planned. Thanks, Maida, for saying this was the wrong day to refuse a dog...

"There's a long list of people I should thank, but right now I need to ask for a favor. What I need most is some quiet time with my family. So if I don't call friends for awhile, please understand it's because we need time to get

214

used to being together again. It's a different world, and we've all gone through some major changes."

Sport was lying with his nose between his paws as if he was praying, and Mickey wished he could also thank Solomon as he said, "I'd appreciate it if everyone could swallow their questions for a while. The truth is I wouldn't know how to answer. Too much happened up there. We didn't know what day it was, or even what month. Only the season... summer, fall, oh-god winter, and finally spring.

"There was a time when I thought that the whole experience -- from waking up in the cave to the day when a snow shelter nearly buried us alive -- might be a transition between dying and whatever would come next... heaven, immortality. There were times when I shouted to the forest that Sport and I were immortal and nothing could kill us.

"I have no answers, only one request. Give us time to separate the dreams from the reality. I'll never call our trip a nightmare, because some of it was beautiful beyond words. The truth is I can never make you see what I saw...

"There are other things I need to try and forget, which I will never talk about. So please, just let me be with my family so we'll know for sure that I really am home."

Sport stood up and his bark was like an Amen.

The applause that started in waves grew to a roar that sounded like Miracle Falls. Relieved to be able to escape back into his house, Mickey knew if he took this scene personally he could end up with worse than a big head.

***

His homecoming speech was replayed on the national news an hour later and the anchorman added a postscript.

"Mickey Barnes is home at last and an entire nation shares his family's joy. He asked to be allowed some private time with his family and his thoughtful message was well received. The press agrees -- no questions for now. A

*little boy was lost and a self-assured young mountaineer
returned. We wish him peace and happiness. Our questions
will come later.*

*"One gets the feeling that Mickey's answers will be of
interest for years to come. For if indeed the very coherent
Michael Barnes, at the tender age of fifteen, learned the
secret of survival alone in the wilderness -- summer, fall,
oh-god winter and spring -- he has, to say the least, a valuable message to impart to the pampered world we live in.
Goodnight, Mickey, and goodnight America."*

Chuck switched off the TV set as he said, "I'm not
sure if I liked his wrap-up, Mick, but you were supreme."

Allison whispered, "Shh... Michael's asleep."

Glenda said softly, "I'm glad he included Mr. Fields
when he was thanking people, even if the name slipped his
mind. And it's no wonder, with all those people!"

Mickey let them believe that he had fallen asleep on
the living room floor. The sight of his face filling the television screen had given him a headache and he had closed
his eyes to listen to his words. He guessed he had made his
point; they were going to leave him alone for a while.

Charlie chuckled, "Bored by his speech, I'll bet." The
strong drug had worn off and he sounded more like himself
bragging, "Mickey sure knew how to handle that deal."

Chuck drawled, "Well, my little brother was never at a
loss for words, if you remember. Mickey always talked up
a storm, but now he doesn't waste words. It was like he was
building a fire out there, one stick at a time. That's going to
take some getting used to, I want you to know. He makes
me feel like I've become the little brother."

Allison's voice was low and musical, like Solomon's.
"This must be such a strange feeling for all of you. I would
never have known him from your descriptions. Do you
think Sport may have changed that much?"

216

Chuck said soberly, "He knows whose dog he is, even if Mickey insists that's an equal partnership. I wonder if we'll ever know that whole story…"

"Maybe not." Glenda made a firm decision. "We'll ask him to share the beautiful things and help him forget the rest." Gently covering him with an afghan, she added, "I'm not going to worry about him sleeping on the hard floor."

Laughter bubbled inside of Mickey and he sighed to let it go. Beside him, Sport's body was warm and relaxed, pretending that he was asleep too. Sport agreed that home was a lot more complicated than they remembered.

Drifting on the edge of sleep after the lights were out, Mickey thought about getting Natalie Fields' remains out of the cave so her father could plant flowers at her grave. That wouldn't be easy or pleasant, but it had to be done.

A psychotic teenager believed he was Mickey Barnes because he had no loving family of his own. His spirit might heal faster if he and Mickey became blood brothers.

Blaine Kern's wife and children would need help if they had to live on a pension from the National Park service. The key that was sewn into the lining of Mickey's snakeskin wallet could open a door to half a million dollars. It was for a cheap locker like those in a roller rink….

No, it was an ice rink!

Suddenly wide-awake, Mickey knew that the loot from the robbery was in cold storage where Flag had promised to take Gary ice-skating before they left for Hong Kong!

There was probably an ice rink near the scene of the crime, but he wouldn't be able to claim the reward without telling someone in authority how Flag and Gary had died.

It wouldn't pay to go stumbling around in the dark. He needed to make a plan, get organized, and take everything step by step. He wouldn't be operating alone. Chuck would help him, and maybe Allison.

Mr. Fields had proven to be a trustworthy family friend and he might be able to set up a private meeting with the governor of Wyoming. Politicians were always looking for ways to make points with voters and there had been a ton of publicity about one lost kid finding his way home.

Chuck hadn't been kidding when he said that the President might invite Mickey and Sport to the White House. It was easier to picture visiting Solomon Montelani in prison, which would take some explaining....

Only one thing was sure. He wasn't going to waste his time and energy dreaming about what might happen. His education and social life required serious thought, and his adjustment to society was going to require more than a little effort. The truth was that nothing would ever be the same.

Mickey didn't want it to be the same. He had made a solemn promise to learn everything there was to learn about this experience, and it wouldn't be over until his name was written on a stone marker with the final date a long time from now. The fact that Sport would be with him until he grew up the rest of the way would assure him of enjoying more happiness than most men ever found in a lifetime.

About the Author:

Betsy Goodspeed's first story was circulated in a TB Sanitarium where the patients' entertainment was limited to listening to the radio. Informed by her doctor that she would 'never sing again' Betsy returned to performing eighteen months later where she met and married her television cameraman.

After the birth of her three children she hosted shows in LA, Denver, and Indianapolis where she also sang and played the harp. Drafting novels during the hours she spent in beauty parlors, writing fiction was a way of re-evaluating reality. Publishing was not a consideration until she interviewed an author who advised, "Writers should start to submit their work as soon as it ceases to embarrass them."

That seemed a worthy goal and Betsy is grateful to her agent, Barbara Deal, for submitting four of her novels before she decided to self-publish. It can take two years for a book to appear in print after being accepted by a publisher, whereas the time can be shortened to a month by self-publishing. The title and cover art are controlled by the publisher, as well as how the words lay on the page. The latter may seem trivial until you think about how important this is to a poet.

The final bonus is that the author's family can participate in the project from editing to the final layout. The cover art for *The Reluctant Mountaineer* was provided by grandson Jorden Goodspeed.

Contact Home2media to learn about future releases of novels by <u>*Betsy*</u> *Goodspeed as well as CDs of her music.*